"You're A Master Of Seduction, Jackson Locke," Lily Said.

"I'm not going to seduce you," he said softly. "I just want to know your secret."

"My secret?" Her heart kicked a little, and not just because of the way he looked.

He tugged gently at her hair. "Your secret. I know you have one."

"Everyone has secrets, Jack."

"I mean the secret you are trying so hard to hide. There's something about your past that makes you evasive. And tonight, you're going to tell me what it is. Now, as a matter of fact."

All she could do was stare at him. Because when she opened her mouth, the truth was going to come out and she was going to tell him the one thing she'd never admitted to anyone.

And that, she realized with a wallop of her heart, was his *real* secret weapon.

Dear Reader,

I'm a makeover junkie. Extreme, subtle, wardrobes, homes, body parts—I love 'em all. In magazines I go straight to the befores and afters. On TV, I lose hours watching some stylist rip apart a career girl's closet and redefine her. Not because I want to see someone squirm over their fashion faux pas, but because I am thrilled by the transformation of a duckling all too comfortable in her own feathers into a work of art, gliding along like a swan. The best changes occur to those who are utterly certain they don't need them, only to end up with a change of clothes and a change of heart.

That's what inspired me to write *His Style of Seduction*. Jackson Locke—a man many readers met in my Silhouette Desire novel *The Sins of His Past*—is a hero so utterly at home and successful in his unconventional, rebellious, creative bad-boy skin that the idea of renovating him is simply laughable. But it's not so funny when he realizes a friend's life hangs in the balance if he doesn't climb into a perfect, corporate mold that will chafe and possibly destroy him. And since the agent of change is a beautiful, tempting woman with her eyes on the prize, Jack uses *everything* he has to distract and derail…and seduce…Lily Monroe.

Writing Jackson Locke's reluctant transformation from lusty bad boy to lifelong lover made me smile, sigh and even shed a tear. I hope it does the same for you.

xoxo
Roxanne St. Claire

ROXANNE
ST. CLAIRE

HIS STYLE
OF
SEDUCTION

Silhouette®
Desire

Published by Silhouette Books
America's Publisher of Contemporary Romance

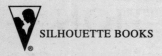

SILHOUETTE BOOKS

ISBN-13: 978-0-373-76841-7
ISBN-10:   0-373-76841-9

HIS STYLE OF SEDUCTION

Visit Silhouette Books at www.eHarlequin.com

Printed in U.S.A.

Books by Roxanne St. Claire

Silhouette Desire

Like a Hurricane #1572
The Fire Still Burns #1608
When the Earth Moves #1648
The Highest Bidder #1681
The Sins of His Past #1702
The Intern Affair #1747
The CEO's Scandalous Affair #1807
His Style of Seduction #1841

ROXANNE ST. CLAIRE

is an award-winning, national bestselling author of nearly twenty romance and suspense novels. A three-time RITA® Award nominee, Roxanne is also a recipient of a Maggie Award, a Booksellers Best Award, an Aspen Gold Award and multiple Awards of Excellence, as well as a CataRomance Reviewers Choice Award for Best Silhouette Desire book. Prior to launching a career as a full-time novelist with the publication of her first book in 2003, Roxanne spent nearly two decades as a public relations and marketing executive. She lives with her husband on the east coast of Florida, where she writes every minute that her preteen and teenaged children are not in school, playing baseball, dancing or otherwise demanding her attention. She loves to hear from readers through e-mail at roxannestc@cfl.rr.com or through snail mail, care of the Space Coast Authors of Romance, P.O. Box 410787, Melbourne, FL, 32941. Please visit her Web site at www.roxannestclaire.com to read excerpts, win prizes and find out more about Roxanne and her books.

This book is dedicated to my Silhouette Books editor, Wanda Ottewell, who loved Jackson Locke even before I did. Wanda is everything a writer could want in an editor or, for that matter, in the heroes we both love: intelligent, humorous, patient, subtle, appreciative and, above all, a true romantic at heart.

One

"I don't want to win awards, dude. I want to sell little red sports cars to sexy young women. How hard can that be?" Jackson Locke trotted down the first two steps of a winding central staircase, his attention on his bare feet as they navigated the high-sheen polish of the wood, his brain flipping through various slogans and discarding them just as fast.

"But what'll I tell the client?" the account exec whined on the other end of his cell phone. "It's eight o'clock on Friday night and he's still sitting in the conference room refusing to move until he talks to you or Mr. Wilding himself about this commercial."

"Forget Reggie. He should be in the air on his way to Nantucket," Jack said. "That is, if he can even get here in this storm."

"He left the office at five. He's running really late."

"What a surprise." Reggie Wilding's hours were legendary. He was the first to arrive at the offices of Wild Marketing and generally the last to leave. But then, that was his name on the door—or part of his name.

"Listen," Jack continued. "Tell the client you talked to the creative director and *I* say that the ending stays, the blonde stays, the dog stays, the tagline stays and, trust me, the sexy babes will—" He froze as his gaze moved from his feet to the foyer below, then he released a silent whistle of air. "Show up when you least expect them."

"What?" The account exec sounded baffled. "Is that a new slogan or something?"

"No. You handle this, man. I gotta run."

He flipped the phone closed and slid it into his jeans pocket as he studied the back of a rain-soaked woman and a sizable suitcase, both trickling water over Mrs. Slattery's precious pine floors. The woman exchanged money with a cabbie, who was just as wet, but grinning at her as though she were some kind of mermaid that had just floated up from Nantucket Sound.

It wasn't unusual for Wild Marketing to haul in an outsider or two for the creative brainstorming weekends held at Reggie's Nantucket Island second home. But Reggie generally warned Jack ahead of time if someone who wasn't part of their small but colorful ad agency staff would be attending.

And he had definitely not been warned about this addition. In fact, Reggie had been uncharacteristically quiet about the whole agenda for the weekend.

Was this the reason?

Tucking a fallen strand of hair behind his ears, he continued his descent, slowing his steps to time his last for the moment she turned around. Until then, he'd enjoy the rear view.

Midnight-black hair plastered over squared, narrow shoulders and fell halfway down her back. What was probably once a nice-looking winter-white dress had turned gray with rainwater and molded to every lethal curve on a long, lean body. Through the magic of moisture, he could see straight through the soaked material and could make out…nothing. She was wearing a thong or…not. Either way—

A bolt of white lightning smacked down to the black water of Nantucket harbor, visible in the distance through the open door.

What kind of campaign were they concocting this weekend, anyway? Didn't Reggie say they might be pitching a sportswear company?

Oh, of course. She was a model. And from the shape of her, he'd put his money on the most elite of the species: a swimsuit model.

He resisted the urge to look skyward in gratitude. Sometimes the advertising gods were too good to him.

Just as he reached the last step, she closed the door behind the cabbie, turned around and met his gaze with a tiny gasp that might have been an echo of his.

Definitely a model. And definitely a gift from the gods, with hand-carved cheekbones, creamy translucent skin and a mouth designed to eat the camera. Among other things. The rain had smeared a bit of makeup under her eyes, giving her a haunting, mysterious look. He let his gaze travel down the revealing wet linen, already visualizing the layout of the ad…. She'd be on the beach, a sliver of something tropical barely covering high, firm breasts, her eyes dark with a hungry invitation. The tagline…Swimwear That Seduces.

Okay, so maybe the copy needed a little work.

She tore him right out of his creative reverie with her question. "Are you here to take my bags?"

"Only if they're going to my room."

Eyes the color of cobalt glass sparkled, and for one heart-stopping instant he thought she'd say yes.

She lifted a strand of hair and pushed it over her shoulder, evidently unfazed by her appearance.

"Let me take a wild guess," she said, her voice low and sultry and, considering her current sodden state, pretty damn confident. "You—" she pointed a single finger at his face "—are not the housekeeper."

He laughed, using the excuse to linger over her curves again. Definitely a bikini body. "Would you believe the pool boy?" he asked.

She gave him a quizzical look, a hint of a smile lighting her eyes before it got to her mouth. "You're kidding."

"Usually." He took the last step and held out his hand. "But I do have the power to bribe Mrs. Slattery, who *is* the housekeeper, to give you the room next to mine."

He deliberately held her cool, damp fingers for the duration of a thunder rumble.

"Are you sure Mrs. Slattery takes bribes?" She glanced around and lowered her voice to a stage whisper. "I called from the airport and she seemed kind of stiff and New Englandy, if you know what I mean."

He tried to look offended. "I'm from New England, and

I'm not stiff." A trickle of rainwater meandered down her breastbone and straight into her cleavage. "Not always, anyway."

She pulled back. "You're kidding again," she said.

"No, I'm not. I was born just thirty miles across that Sound." He indicated the view he'd just seen out the front door. "Raised over there in Cape Cod."

"Ah, Cape *Cahd*." She drawled out the last syllable and nodded knowingly. "Now I hear the accent."

"A model *and* a linguist?"

That earned a quick laugh. "Neither. I'm Lily Harper and I'm here as the guest of Mr. Wilding."

He regarded her closely. She didn't flinch at the examination, regardless of the fact that her makeup had run and her hair looked like a mop dipped in India ink. Who *was* this woman? "Reggie's never mentioned a Lily Harper."

"Maybe Mr. Wilding's keeping me a secret." She shrugged. "Wouldn't be the first time."

The first time? "You're really not a model?"

"You're really not the pool boy?"

He laughed, taking a step closer to inhale the rain on her, mixed with something spicy and sharp. "So what brings you to the weekend brainstorm, Lily Harper? Are you with a research firm? A focus group? A prospective client?"

She gave her head a quick shake. "None of the above. How about you?"

"I'm the creative director of Wild Marketing. Without me, there is no brainstorm."

"Ah." She raked him with a long, slow appraisal that sent all sorts of red blood cells racing south to wake up the boys for a possible party. "So you're the infamous Jackson Locke."

"I prefer *legendary*."

That made her laugh. Not quick, this time. A slow, throaty chuckle that revealed perfect white teeth and a hint of dimples. A laugh that sounded like pure sex.

"Maybe there isn't going to be any brainstorm," she said, then looked away, suddenly making a keen study of the high ceilings, the casually elegant Nantucket-style living room to her right, and a formal dining room to the left of the center hall. "Nice place, isn't it?"

"Of course there's going to be a brainstorm," he assured her.

It really didn't matter why she'd been invited. Whatever Reggie had planned would be revealed in time. In the meantime…Jack could play.

He picked up her suitcase and laid a possessive hand on her lower back. "Why don't we find out where your home base is, and get you out of those clothes?"

She paused midstep and killed him with one look.

"Into something dry," he added.

"You're a cool one, Jackson Locke. I doubt you really need my services."

His mind whirled through the possibilities of what her services could be, landing on…nothing Reggie would condone on a weekend dedicated to the business.

"Cool, huh?" he asked, dipping a little close to her ear to whisper, "Of course, I can do hot, if that'll get me some services."

"I bet you can," she said softly, looking up at him with those blueberry eyes. "But Mr. Wilding probably has something else in mind."

Reggie Wilding was the boss, conservative as hell, and

one of the truest friends a man could have. Reg must have a damn good reason for inviting sharp-talking, great-looking, nice-smelling Lily Harper. And Jack wasn't about to question the wisdom of his mentor.

Just then, Dorothea Slattery barreled out of the kitchen and into the hall, ignoring Jack and narrowing steel-gray eyes that perfectly matched the streaks in her wiry hair. "Miss Harper! I apologize for keeping you waiting."

"No apology necessary," Lily said with a smile. "I've only just arrived."

The housekeeper beamed at Jack, reassuring him that she was still his biggest fan. "Oh, thank you, Mr. Jack, for taking care of her. I'm afraid I have some very bad news."

"What's that?"

She let out an exaggerated sigh. "First of all, Mr. Wilding called and they have shut the Nantucket airport completely. This storm is only going to get worse and he won't be here until tomorrow."

"That's too bad," Lily said.

"That's fine," Jack said at exactly the same time.

They exchanged a quick look, but the housekeeper continued, "But I'm so sorry that I cannot stay to serve you dinner. The power's gone out on the other side of the island and I have to get to my father to set up his generator. He's on oxygen."

"Of course," Lily said, moving toward the woman with an outstretched hand. "You go. We'll be fine."

"Do you need me to take you over there, Mrs. S?"

Mrs. Slattery clasped her hands together and gazed at him with adoring eyes. "Oh, thank you, no, Mr. Jack. You are so good to me. But I can drive in this rain."

"Are any of the other Wild Marketers here yet?" Jack asked. "I can get things started even if Reggie can't come until tomorrow."

Mrs. Slattery looked from one to the other, then frowned again, her expression unsure. "There is no one else here this weekend, Mr. Jack. Didn't Mr. Wilding tell you that?"

Jack almost dropped the bag. "No, he didn't."

But Lily, he noticed, didn't seem at all surprised.

"I left an assortment of dinner selections in the kitchen," Mrs. Slattery said. "And there's wine and dessert and—"

"Please," Lily insisted. "Go take care of your father. We'll be fine."

"Absolutely fine," Jack reassured her. "Don't worry about us. Just let me know where I should take this bag."

Mrs. Slattery pointed straight up the stairs. "She's across the hall from you, Mr. Jack."

He resisted the urge to kiss his favorite housekeeper, who had just confirmed what he *never* took for granted: Jackson Locke lived a charmed existence.

He didn't know.

Lily shut the door to her guest room, and leaned against the cool wood, closing her eyes. Jackson Locke really didn't know why she was there. If he had, surely he would have mentioned it after she'd made the comment about her services.

Evidently Reggie Wilding wanted the element of surprise on his side.

Her hand on the brass knob, she briefly considered turning the lock. But that was crazy. He was a grade-A flirt, but she didn't think he was the type to force his way into her personal space with six feet two inches of charm and sex appeal. Not to mention all that tangled honey hair that grazed his jaw, and eyes the shade of freshly cut grass, and just as inviting.

Lily took a much-needed deep breath.

The man taxed every skill of self-possession she'd ever mastered. And she'd mastered quite a few. Including whatever it took to play Olympic-quality verbal volleyball when she looked like a rat who'd just hoisted herself through a sewer grate.

But that wasn't why she needed a calming breath. Was it possible Reggie Wilding had not bothered to inform his right-hand man and creative director that the agency was up for sale? And the buyer was about to sign on the dotted line…as soon as one simple change was made?

Although how anyone could call a complete and total makeover of Jackson Locke *simple* was beyond her.

He was, in fact, a man so unlikely to embrace the idea of a personal and professional makeover that it was laughable that someone would even try. Still, that's what Reggie Wilding wanted, and the fee he'd offered would pay her office rent for three months…taking her three months closer to her dreams.

Lily shook her head and flipped open her suitcase, remembering the day Reggie had walked into her office and announced he'd been referred to her by a very happy client of her burgeoning professional makeover business.

When he asked if she'd be willing to conduct the project on Nantucket Island, she didn't even consider saying no. Even though the transformation of a top ad-agency creative guy into a textbook, classic executive was pushing her image consulting skills to a new level. Before this, her clients had consisted of college grads on the interview circuit and a few ambitious administrative types who were longing to break in to management.

But this? This could put The Change Agency on the map, and, even better, could start Lily on the path to the freedom and security she longed for.

Still…what could she do to improve a man like Jackson Locke?

Okay, a haircut. Although she liked the nearly shoulder-length golden-brown mess that fell over his eye when he dipped his head to whisper a one-liner. Maybe just a closer shave. But the stubble over that square jaw looked so…alluring.

Shoes.

Yes. They could start with shoes. But what Reggie had in mind…oh, that would never fly with *the pool boy*.

So she had tonight to get to know him. To plan a strategy for her success. To find out what was important to him and convince him that a little personal renovation could be the best thing for him to achieve his goals. Surely he had professional aspirations. Who didn't?

Seizing her cell phone from her handbag, she flipped it open to call Reggie and confirm exactly what Jack knew.

No service.

Of course not, in this storm. Well, she'd just work on that art of saying nothing she'd learned in a management workshop she'd attended. Until Reggie showed up, she'd have to handle Jack on her own.

Oh, like that would be unpleasant.

An unholy blast of sexual heat shot through her. Ignoring it, she grabbed her cosmetic bag and headed to the shower, admiring the Wedgwood-blue-painted furniture and the comfy throw rugs that added to the seaside charm of the supersize summer home. In the bathroom she refused to dally with even a glance in the mirror.

However bad she looked, Jack had made her feel… good. Really good. A tingle twisted through her as she stripped, cranked up the shower and stepped into the hot stream of water to wash the rain away with shampoo and body gel that smelled like the ocean.

A flash of white lightning lit everything for an instant, and a near-simultaneous boom of thunder shook the glass of the shower door. Startled, Lily reached for the taps to turn off the water and get out, just as the lights flickered on and off and on…then complete blackness enveloped the room.

Her heart thudding, she leaned into the water stream to feel the wall for the faucets. Once she had them in her hands, she turned both to the left with a forceful jerk and the spray stopped.

But the darkness was total. All she could hear was the rain on the roof and windows. Everything else was buried in quiet and black. She blinked, but her eyes still hadn't adjusted and she might as well have been wearing a blindfold.

Damn. Why hadn't she hung out a towel or a robe? She tried to mentally re-create the layout of the bathroom, which she hadn't bothered to study. Were there towels on a rack above the sink? In a closet?

She slid the shower glass to the left as she heard the creak of the guest-room door.

"Lily? Are you okay?"

Jack.

"I'm fine." Naked, wet and unable to see past her nose, but fine. Oh, and she'd left the bathroom door wide open. Not that he could see her, but still…

"We lost power," he announced.

"I gathered that." From the shower, she felt the wall for a shelf. Her hand landed on the smooth porcelain top of the toilet tank.

"I wanted to make sure you were safe. That strike was really close."

"I'm…in the shower. But I'm all right." She slid her hand until she touched something hard and round, but it toppled out of her reach and smashed to the floor with the crash of splintering glass. Lily swore softly.

"What was that?" Jack's voice was louder. He'd come into the bedroom.

"I knocked something over. There's probably glass all over the floor."

"Don't move," he said. "I'll get a flashlight. But don't get out of the shower or you'll get cut."

She blew out a breath and an unfamiliar sense of helplessness took hold. "You be careful, too. Are you still barefoot?"

Was that a rumble of thunder or his laugh? "You don't miss a thing, huh?"

No, she didn't. And that's what she was paid to do. "Just hurry, Jack. I'm getting cold." She shut the shower door again.

"Hang on, I have an idea." In a moment she heard a soft *whoof* and gentle thump. "Okay, sweetheart. It's safe to come out now."

She drew back, realizing he was right on the other side of the shower door. "Safe?"

"I laid a throw rug from the bedroom on the floor," he explained. "There's no glass on it."

"That was imaginative."

"I'm the creative director, remember? Imagination is my...second greatest attribute."

She laughed lightly. "Your first would be humility?"

"That's third."

She shook her head, still smiling. "Go away now, and I'll get out and find a towel."

"Go away?" He sounded insulted.

"Yes, *go away*. I'm not wearing anything."

"Including shoes. I'll guide you to the bedroom so you don't accidentally go off this carpet and slice your foot with glass. I can't see either, but I know how big the carpet is and where I've laid it."

"In other words, this is not your evil scheme to see me naked."

"That comes later."

Water snaked down her spine at the same time as a zing of anticipation raced up her tummy. She touched the shower door handle. "I'd say close your eyes, but—"

"You know I won't."

She slid the glass wider, inch by agonizing inch. Still, the darkness was complete and she couldn't see anything at all. "All right. Where are you?"

"Right here." His hand closed around hers. Could he see her? Did he have some kind of night vision that she didn't?

She sucked in a little breath at the warmth that emanated from him. Heat seemed to cloak his skin. Along with an earthy, manly scent that somehow mixed perfectly with the ocean aroma of the shower gel.

In one step, she could press her naked body against that powerful chest. Run her shower-soaked fingers through that mane of golden silk. Arousal blasted through her and her nipples, already budded from the chill, ached with a rush of blood and the undeniably erotic thought that he might see her, might touch her.

"Come on, sweetheart," he urged, tugging her hand gently. "Unless you want me to climb in there with you."

"You're bad, Jack Locke."

"Actually, I'm very, very—" The light flashed so blindingly white that she gasped. In the endless, timeless instant that they were suspended in illumination, all she could see were his eyes widening and dropping to her body, his gaze as hot as the lightning, his fingers tightening their grip on her hand.

And then the velvet blackness descended again.

She waited through the thunder, expecting a quip. The sly remark. The banter that he used as efficiently as a pirate with his sword.

But he only let out a long, slow breath, as though he needed it to steady himself.

"Lily," he whispered as the rumble silenced. "You're gorgeous."

Nothing could have undone her more effectively.

Her hammering heart sent liquid heat through her veins, so she took her own steadying breath, lifted her left leg and found solid ground on his homemade safety mat.

"Don't move from this spot," he instructed, "or you might step on glass. I'll look for a towel under the sink."

As if she was in a position to argue.

"Here we go," he said after a moment.

She reached out for the towel, but instead her hands landed on the solid planes of his chest as he closed his arms around her, wrapping the towel around her back.

Grasping the terry-cloth ends at her chest, he drew her one step closer to him and closed the towel around her.

She could see shadows now. She could make out the angles of his jaw, the shape of his mouth, the soft wave in the long hair that framed his face.

His eyes locked on to her and he tugged that towel, and her, closer.

His lips parted. Lily's chest nearly burst as her pounding heart and trapped breath warred for space and release.

"Don't you know it's dangerous to take a shower during a thunderstorm?" he asked, a tease and gentle warning in his voice. "You could have been electrocuted."

Which couldn't burn any more than his voice, his touch, his very warm body. "I took a chance," she admitted.

"You like to take chances, Lily?" The question was so loaded with double entendre she almost laughed.

"No," she managed to say. "I prefer to have control." *Right.* Then why was she standing there, arms at her sides, letting him manipulate the situation with one well-placed fist? All he had to do was open his fingers and she'd be naked and trapped by those sea-green eyes.

Fire sizzled straight through her, melting her bones and curling her toes at the thought. She lifted her face toward his, aching to taste his mouth on hers. But he merely took her hand, lifted it to her chest and gave her the ends of the towel to hold. Keeping her little cover on was now her job, not his.

"There. Now you have control."

Not exactly.

"You know, for a minute there, I thought you were going to kiss me," she admitted.

He laughed softly and disappeared into the darkness, although he was no farther than two feet away. "Now you know my secret weapon," he said quietly. "I never do what people expect."

And that's precisely why changing Jack Locke would be one hell of a challenge.

That, and the fact that if he hadn't transferred the control back to her hand, if he had leaned down and kissed her, she would have done nothing to stop him.

"Sam?"

She didn't know Saint Samantha Wilding? "Reggie's wife."

"I've never met her." There was nothing but honesty in her voice.

So Reggie picked this flower all by himself? Wowzer, Reg. Jack's already sky-high respect for the older man increased exponentially.

"She's a good lady," he told her as they rounded the hand-carved banister newel at the bottom of the steps. "She should have had twenty kids, but didn't have any. Treats me like her very own son. We're going straight back to the kitchen now."

He tightened his grasp on her fingers and guided her toward the back of the sprawling house. Every corner remained bathed in an eerie darkness, with only the occasional lightning, and even that had seemed to slow a bit. The steady rain had lessened to a soft staccato against the windows.

Let's get to it, Lily. "So if you don't know Sam, and you're not here for business, how do you know Reggie?"

"A client referral." Her tone left no room for questions. End of discussion.

But he knew every client of Wild Marketing. "Which one?"

"You know, I'm not exactly sure who referred me."

All right, so she was in on the setup and playing coy. But still, she'd packed her bags, got on a plane, braved the elements and taken a chance on meeting him. Was she in the market for Mr. Right? Too bad if she was.

However, if she was shopping for Mr. Have a Really Good Time on a Rainy Weekend, then she'd found her man.

He studied her in the soft artificial light and realized that...the battery in the flashlight was dying a slow but very real death.

Then it would be dark again. Who cared? There was no business to worry about, no brainstorming to distract them, just one elaborate *blind date*. Jack was free to flirt, fool around and take this as far as she was willing to go.

The gods, every flippin' one of them, were so good to him he could cry.

"Oh, here's the wine Mrs. S. mentioned." He shone the dimming light on an excellent bottle of Château de La Tour, with two sparkling crystal wineglasses and a corkscrew thoughtfully left out for them. "I'm not sure, but it looks like the good stuff."

She let out a quick breath as she peered at the label. "I'll say."

"Reggie must want us to be extremely, uh, comfortable."

"I don't know," Lily said with a smile in her voice. "I think Mrs. Slattery is secretly in love with you and she raided the wine cellar for the best she could find."

"You think?"

Lily chuckled and started a slow prowl around the kitchen. "She all but threw her arms around you to kiss you when you offered to drive her to her father's house."

Yep. And then, conveniently, had to disappear. He balanced the flashlight on the counter, so that it spilled an umbrella of light over them, and pointed what was left of its ray directly to the ceiling.

"Don't worry. She's not my type."

"I'm not worried."

At her matter-of-fact tone, he glanced at her, then started

the process of uncorking the wine. "Can you see well enough? Do you think you can find what she's left us to eat?"

"Maybe." In the shadows she moved to the double doors of a Sub-Zero refrigerator. She pulled the door open, but of course it was dark inside, so she closed it. "I need the flashlight. I don't want to leave the door open for long and let all the cold air out. We don't know how long we'll be without electricity."

The cork slipped out with a hollow pop. "Let's have wine first, then we'll forage for food." Surely a little bit of La Tour would get the truth out of her. She'd admit she was Reggie's niece or neighbor or the daughter of a country club acquaintance sent in for a weekend of potential romance.

"I'll have some," she said, scooping the flashlight off the counter. "But with food."

This lady definitely liked to call the shots. "Whatever you prefer," he said, pouring two glasses without benefit of light. Some things he could do in the dark. Most things, in fact.

She aimed the light inside the fridge. "Oh, a beautiful tomato and mozzarella salad."

"Mrs. S. is a genius."

"And some shrimp cocktail."

"Her specialty."

She stuck the flashlight between her teeth and used it like a miner's lamp, leaning into the fridge to pull out a tray. "Aah ah ah-ah ah-ah," she mumbled around the cylinder.

He chuckled and ambled behind her with the glasses of wine. "I don't speak flashlight, sweetheart." He set one glass on the counter and slid the flashlight out of her mouth.

"I said 'and some pasta salad.'" She reached back into

the fridge and he stood behind her, the light just bright enough for him to make out the silhouette of a sweet round bottom jutting toward him. Her T-shirt had ridden up to reveal some butter-smooth flesh and a precious little dip in her lower back. His throat went bone-dry at the temptation she unknowingly offered.

Then she stood and turned, and his breath caught at how pretty she was in the dimly lit kitchen, damp tendrils of long dark hair curling around a face completely devoid of makeup.

Beautiful. Natural. Confident.

How did Reggie know exactly, precisely, right down to the dimples—top and bottom—what Jack liked in a woman? And then how could his boss be so sly as to not breathe a word in advance, knowing that happily single Jack would have found some highly creative reason to be a no-show?

Sometimes Reggie knew Jack better than Jack knew himself. This would be one of those times.

He stepped back as Lily glided efficiently through the ever-darkening kitchen, letting her rummage through drawers and cabinets for plates, silverware and napkins.

"The flashlight's fading," he said, taking a pass at a few drawers himself. "But I can't find candles and matches."

"Okay. We can eat fast. I'll just set us up at the bar." She set two places at the granite counter that lined the center island.

"Do we actually need place settings?" he said, a little incredulity in his laugh. "I mean, this pretty much qualifies as an emergency situation, don't you think?"

"I never eat without a proper place setting," she responded, leveling him with a cool look.

Well, la-di-da. "I don't think you're going to worry

about place mats when that battery dies," he said. "But suit yourself. And here." He slipped the glass of wine into her hand. "You haven't had a sip yet. Let's toast."

She smiled and took the glass, the dim uplighting making shadows in her chiseled features.

"Thank you," she responded, holding the wineglass toward him. "Here's to…"

"Thunderstorms," he said.

"And to getting power," she countered.

He started to take a sip and paused. "Power? Yeah, I bet you like to have that in a relationship."

She regarded him over the rim of her glass. "I meant *electricity*."

"Oh, sweetheart, we've got plenty of that." He touched his rim to hers and let the ring of crystal hum in their ears. He waited until the glass reached her mouth, just until the wine neared her lips. Then he said, "You can stop the charade now, Lily. We both know exactly why you're here."

She choked before a drop of wine could have touched her lips. "We do?"

He sipped his wine, locked on her stunned expression. Then he set the wineglass on the counter and gently took hers out of her hand, putting it next to his. "And would you like to know what I think about it?"

She swallowed, but he could tell it was an effort. "I can only imagine what you think about it."

He reached up and placed his hands on her shoulders, gently rubbing his thumbs over the thin fabric of her T-shirt. "I don't know why you didn't level with me from the minute you arrived."

She narrowed skeptical navy blue eyes at him. "I think

Reggie wants to be the one to level with you, Jack. He wasn't sure you'd like the idea."

He tunneled his fingers into the still-damp hair at the nape of her neck, watching her eyes widen as he eased her closer to him.

"I like the idea because I like you." He inched his face closer to hers. "In fact, tomorrow morning, when we wake up together, right after we have a few hours of wall-shaking, earth-quaking, brain-rattling sex, let's give Reggie a call and tell him how brilliant he is."

Just as her jaw slackened and her mouth opened, he captured her lips with his, sharing the vanilla-and-oak flavor of the wine and closing his eyes to enjoy the sweetest taste he could ever remember.

When he opened his eyes, the flashlight had gone dark.

Time stopped. Breathing stopped. Her heart stopped.

But nothing—and no one—stopped that kiss.

Lily was too far from the counter to reach back for support, so she slid her hands over Jack's amazing shoulders, leaned into his mouth and held on for the ride.

Her stomach dipped, her legs trembled and a slow burn heated her from the inside out.

His fingers threaded into her hair, angling her head as he launched a second roller coaster of a kiss, this time taking her tongue along as a passenger.

Instinct took over as she rose on her toes, urging her stomach right into the hard ridge of his erection. He tightened his fingers in her hair and invaded her mouth, a soft moan rumbling in his chest as he pressed himself against her.

"Lily." Her name was no more than a breath of air as

his hands glided down her back and settled hot and warm on the bare skin of her waist.

She finally opened her eyes. It was pitch-dark again.

"Oh," she muttered, still unable to separate from the sheer pleasure of full body contact. "We lost our battery."

He dropped his hands a little lower, resting on the rise of her backside as he eased her bottom against him. "But we still have all this electricity, sweetheart." He feathered her cheek and ear with airy kisses. "We don't need no stinkin' flashlight."

She couldn't help but laugh. "How can you make jokes at a time like this?" she whispered, still incapable of extricating herself from his hands and body. "We're completely in the dark. At the mercy of the elements. All we can do is *feel* our way around."

"Yep." He slid his hands up her waist, lingering on her rib cage, inches from her breasts. "And it feels good." He eased her back against the counter and tormented her with some more direct contact with his rock-hard arousal.

"Jack…" She tilted her head and let him nibble at her neck, the ability to slow him down slipping from her grasp with each sizzling touch of his lips and tongue and hips. "This might not be such a good idea…."

"I told you, baby, this is a great idea." His kisses burned a trail over her throat, down her breastbone and over the cotton of her T-shirt. She could feel the heat of his lips through the fabric, making her breasts tingle and ache.

She forced her brain into gear. *This* wasn't the idea he liked. Was it? Wasn't he talking about her assignment to…renovate him into an ad-agency president?

She placed her hands on his chest and nudged him back,

the room still so dark that she could see only the whites of his eyes and gleam of his flawless smile. "Jack," she whispered. "Listen to me."

A soft moan of disappointment caught in his throat, but he stilled his hands and eased up the pressure against her body.

"Do you really know why Reggie sent me here?"

He released a soft, knowing laugh. "How long did you think it would take me to figure it out, Lily? No one else is here, no creative client problems are on the agenda. Hell, there *is* no agenda. Just you." He skimmed his hands along her ribs again. "And me." He grazed the sides of her breasts, torturing her with the possibilities.

"And you don't hate the whole idea?" she asked. "I mean, Reggie wasn't sure you'd go for it, and now that I've met you, I can tell why he thought you'd be...difficult to convince."

A rumble of laughter in his chest vibrated hers. "You should have more confidence, sweetheart. I think you're fantastic."

"But...what about...the whole concept of...changing you? You'll go for that?"

He stiffened just enough for her to know it wouldn't be an easy battle. Then he relaxed against her, easing his hips into hers.

"Let's worry about all that tomorrow, okay? There's plenty of time to discuss...the future. I'm more interested in tonight. In this." He settled his mighty erection against her stomach and sent a line of fire up and down her spine. "In now."

Her night vision had improved enough for her to see into his eyes. Was he sincere? Did he really not care about her mission? But then he helped himself to another slow, hot, wet kiss, and everything came to a screeching halt again, except her ability to do anything other than…kiss back.

"Nature's playing games with us, Lily," he whispered. "First she turned out the lights." Slowly, leisurely, his hands rounded her breasts until his palms covered her aching nipples. "Then she gave us the music of the rain." He grazed the points with his fingertips and more fire shot through her. "And all we need to do…" He rolled his hips from side to side, slow and easy, nice and hard. "Is dance in the dark."

She shuddered. This was seduction. The most elemental, obvious and relentless seduction she'd ever experienced…and the effect was dizzying. As fast and deadly as a lightning bolt, he'd short-circuited her brain, fried her common sense and left her absolutely no ability to see beyond the next few hours.

"You like this, Lily?" he asked, sliding one hand under her T-shirt to caress the fabric of her bra. "You like when I touch you?"

She managed a pitiful "Uh-huh" as he dropped one hot finger along the waistband of her yoga pants, gliding from front to back, where his whole palm settled in to cover her backside.

"You wanna dance in the dark with me, Lily?" His voice was so low and so sure and so sexy that she simply trembled. "I promise you'll like it."

"This wasn't…exactly the first night I had in mind," she said, her argument sounding as weak as her knees felt.

"Sometimes, when it's right, things happen fast." He fluttered his fingertips over her nipple. "Or slow." He rubbed her breast in his palm. "Tonight it's your choice."

Tomorrow, business would take front and center again. But… "Tonight," she murmured into his kiss and felt him smile in response.

"Now," he added, giving her the thrill of weightlessness as he lifted her feet off the ground and slowly whirled her in a half circle. "Pick your dance floor, baby," he said with a soft, seductive kiss. "Here in the kitchen? Out in the living room? On the billiard table? In the steam room?"

She nearly swooned. "I guess a bedroom's just too damn conventional for a guy like you."

"I can do conventional. On special occasions. There's a guest room in the wing behind the kitchen," he said, gathering her closer in his arms. "I've stayed in it. We can find it in the dark. It'll be an adventure."

"It certainly gives new meaning to the term blind date," she added wryly.

That earned her a quick and hearty laugh and an affectionate squeeze. "I totally get why Reggie thinks we'd work together."

She let out a sigh of relief, grateful that he'd be mature enough to recognize that her role in his business had nothing to do with her role in his bedroom.

And they *would* talk about it tomorrow. But tonight she simply wrapped her arm around his waist, tucked herself into the rock-hard muscles of his body and matched his slow steps toward the inevitable.

"I know there's a guest suite down this hallway." As they turned a corner he paused, one hand outstretched in anticipation of obstacles. He patted his hand along the wall and then stopped. "Ah. Here we go." Slowly he turned the knob and the door creaked open. "Let's dance."

A shiver of anticipation vibrated through her body. As soon as they were in the room, he folded her into his arms and pressed her against the granite of his chest, his heart hammering at exactly the same accelerated rate as hers.

"There might be a candle in here," he said. "Do you want me to look for it?"

"No."

That was all Jack needed to hear. Without waiting for her to take even another breath, he backed her into the room, fairly certain that there was a bed under the one large window. One flash of faraway lightning lit the sheer curtains and proved his memory right.

It was just enough to see the hunger and arousal in her eyes. When her knees hit the bed, he dropped her down on the mattress.

Finesse be damned. He was so hard it hurt and she was so hot it hurt even more. In an instant he had the flimsy T-shirt over her head and he dropped down to taste the rose-tipped breasts that had burned in his memory since the first lightning flash. In one move, he unclipped her bra in the back and flipped the satiny thing out of his way, palming one breast with a firm hand and kissing the other.

She tasted like sea-salted soap and that one drop of wine he'd had. Her nipple swelled in his mouth and kicked his aching erection into higher gear. He licked around the darkened circle and sucked again. From deep inside her chest she mewed in ecstasy, burrowing her fingers into his hair, twisting the locks and pressing his face against her flesh.

She said his name and rocked her hips, then gave his shoulders enough of a firm push that he knew exactly what she wanted.

He nibbled his way down her tight little belly, and curled his tongue into her navel. Her hips rose in response. The workout pants went down in one smooth yank and something tiny and white and lacy was gone in one more.

He crooned softly at the sight of her moist tuft, his mouth already watering, his tongue ready to sample a taste of Lily.

"Jack." She sat up and started to pull at his shirt. "I want to see you. I want to touch you."

He knelt in front of her, stripping off his polo shirt and unsnapping his jeans. She took over and deftly finished the zipper, pushing at the denim. "Let me. Let me."

He held up both hands in surrender. "I'm yours, baby. Just let me grab something from my wallet."

From his jeans pocket he retrieved a condom and dropped it onto the bed next to them, then she got him down to his boxers. As he put his hands on the waistband, she grabbed his wrists.

"I want to undress you."

He chuckled again. "You're the boss, sweetheart." Again he knelt on the bed and sucked in a breath as she took one of his nipples in her mouth. Her fingers splayed over his chest, working the hair, kneading the muscles and groaning with a subtle feminine appreciation. Her nails trailed down his stomach and finally reached the place he wanted her to touch.

Slowly she eased the shorts over the tent of his erection, and as she revealed him, his hard-on intensified under the heat of her gaze.

She closed her eyes, dipped her head and swiped her tongue right over him.

He almost swore at the shock of the pleasure, and somewhere in the distant recesses of his mind he remembered he'd have to find out exactly how Reggie *knew* this woman was made for him.

She stroked him and kissed him and guided him into her mouth. Hungry for her, he eased himself in the opposite direction, kissed her belly, then found the tiny dark triangle between her legs. He licked her once. She bucked and gasped sharply.

The intensity of the exchange was almost too much. Her mouth and her body were so sweet and hot and wet, all he could do was moan and move into her and against her, smelling the tangy essence of a woman who knew exactly what she wanted and how she wanted it. Then took it.

He almost came at the thought of it.

He kissed her thighs, her hips and finally righted himself on top of her.

She picked up the condom, tore the foil with her teeth and handed the latex to him with a sly smile. "Hurry."

"Yes, ma'am." He laughed softly, and in two seconds he was sheathed and seeking the heated moisture of her womanhood, his arms bracing above her, the scent and taste of her sex still invading every pore.

He gave her a quick smile. "Don't tell me. You want the top."

She half laughed, but shook her head, lifting her hips in invitation. "I just want you inside me."

At the declaration, he closed his eyes and entered her with a long, slow, agonizing groan, the insane tightness of her body almost killing him. He thrust once, giving in to the wicked hot pleasure of letting go, and then again, another ragged breath tearing his throat.

He had to slow down. Had to find a way to make this last.

"There," he whispered as they reached a perfect rhythm and he dropped to his elbows. He burrowed deeper, pulled back and slid farther into her sweet body again. "Just like that."

Her eyelids fluttered and her fingers dug into his biceps, but she never lost the rhythm. *Just. Like. That.*

Sweat trickled down his temple and she reached up and wiped it away, snagging his gaze as he plunged into her again.

Her eyes were so beautiful, so wide with wonder and desire and pleasure. He couldn't look away. His chest squeezed, his throat ached and his whole lower half clutched at the sight of her.

"We're gonna be good together, Jack," she whispered, brushing a lock of his hair back, then tucking it behind his ear. "We are. You'll see."

His heart dipped a little at the long-term implication. But considering where they were and what they were doing, even he wasn't arrogant enough to make a joke about Reggie's setup.

"We *are* good together, Lily," he insisted, upping the tempo of their union as though he could prove it. "I already see."

She met him with every stroke, her body slick with moisture and heat, sliding against him like wet satin. He had to bite his lip to keep from totally pounding himself into her.

She closed her eyes and arched her back, still increasing their rhythm.

He clenched his jaw and thrust again. And again. And again. And again.

She turned her head and gripped his hips with her thighs.

Gratification overtook her, as their breathing echoed through the room and he gave in, thrusting himself as far and fast as he could. She shuddered once, then again, then rolled against him without any control, murmuring his name and begging him to join her.

His own control disappeared with hers, as a wild, hot release built up until he spilled himself deep inside her. All the way inside a smart, sexy, sweet-faced woman he still hadn't seen completely dry.

Three

A mechanical stutter. The hum of an air conditioner. The ping of a hallway light.

Power.

From behind Lily, a long, hard body stirred. A large hand closed over her breast. A very masculine muscle prodded her backside. A wholly different kind of power.

Lily closed her eyes and sighed with a bone-deep contentment. The hazy light of dawn danced through sheer curtains, pale enough for her to know it couldn't even be six o'clock yet.

"Did you have sweet dreams, Lily?" His question, accompanied by a soft kiss on her shoulder, sent the hairs on the back of her head prancing up and down.

She moaned with satisfaction and nestled her rear end against his stomach. "I dreamed about food."

He leaned up on one elbow and brushed some hair off her face, then kissed her cheek. "I told you I'd bring us a picnic in the middle of the night. I like shrimp in bed."

She wrinkled her nose.

"Oh, I forgot," he said. "It's not a meal without a napkin and place mat."

"A table helps, too. I'll teach you about all that good stuff."

He eased his hand off her body and moved imperceptibly away. But she was fluent in body language and recognized the signs of discomfort. No, she'd never expected the makeover of Jackson Locke to be easy.

"You know what?" He scooted up. "I'm going to take a quick run."

"A run?" She flipped around to look at him, her breath catching at the sight of all that disheveled burnished-gold hair and the dark shadow of beard on his cheeks. Good God in heaven, how could she even think about turning him into a corporate executive?

Because Reggie Wilding was paying her, for one thing. And if she succeeded, there could be more business like this. Lots more. Then she wouldn't have to worry about rent, but a mortgage. But right now it was hard to think about dreams of security when she was looking at a man who made her think about...sex.

"Yeah, I usually hit the gym in the morning, but here I like to jog on the beach. Wanna come?"

For a moment she considered it. Just to stay near him, just to watch him move. But the storm had stopped and normalcy would be returning to Nantucket. Along with Reggie, no doubt.

She shook her head. "I'll pass. But would you run to the kitchen first and make some coffee?"

"If you can wait, I'll do even better than that and get some designer caffeine for you in town."

"Yum. Caramel latte with a ton of whipped cream." A five-dollar extravagance she rarely indulged.

He wiggled his eyebrows. "We could get very creative with whipped cream."

"Said the creative director." She grinned at him. "Sorry, but I'm not sharing my whipped cream. I like it too much."

His lip quirked up and he reached for her, running a warm hand over her hip and along her thigh. "Thank God you're not a swimsuit model."

She almost snorted. "Why on earth would you even say that?"

"I thought you were when I saw you in the foyer." He squeezed her leg. "You've got the body for it."

"Thanks…I guess. But what would make you think Reggie would invite a swimsuit model this weekend?"

He lifted one of his carved-from-stone shoulders. "Hey, I'm never sure what to expect with Reggie." Then those emerald eyes danced. "But he sure nailed me when he picked you."

She smiled, warmed by the compliment but certain that when they got into the actual process of polishing him to corporate perfection he wouldn't be quite so sweet about it. "We'll see how things go."

He looked relieved. "What do you do, anyway? What's your job?"

Her job? "This is my—" A sudden bang and the sound of solid, determined footsteps in the hall stopped her.

"Reggie!" she whispered, a hint of panic tightening her chest. She was fine with the situation, but how would Reggie feel?

Someone tapped on the door. "Miss Harper? Are you in there?"

Relief washed through her at the sound of Mrs. Slattery's voice, but she automatically put her hand over Jack's mouth and burned him with a warning look. "Just a second," she called, scrambling up and out of the bed.

He regarded her naked body with a mix of amusement and desire. "Should I hide?"

She put one finger to her lips to shush him. "Please. We just met. I don't want her to…" She pointed to the en suite bathroom. "Go in there."

He looked skyward and slowly pushed himself up from the bed. She pulled on her yoga pants and yanked the T-shirt over her head.

When he disappeared into the bathroom, she inched the door open and found Mrs. Slattery waiting patiently.

"Miss Harper, I saw all the glass in your bathroom!" she exclaimed. "You were so smart to come down here to sleep."

Lily nodded and thanked God she wasn't forced to lie. "We lost power in the middle of the night and I accidentally broke something."

"No problem." She held up a work-worn hand. "I've already taken care of it. Were you eating when the electricity went out? The food was left out in the kitchen."

"Uh, yes. Jack was getting dinner when we had the outage. We didn't risk going back there in the dark." Lily kept the door at little more than a crack, half expecting Jack to jump out of the bathroom any minute. "Have you heard from Reggie?"

"He's on his way, miss. I wanted to tell Mr. Jack, but his bedroom door is still closed." Her silvery eyes sparked with affection. "He likes to sleep."

Among other things. "I'll move back up to the other room now, Mrs. Slattery. Thank you for worrying about me and for taking care of that mess."

"Oh, that's fine, dear. Would you like me to make some coffee and biscuits, maybe an omelet? Mr. Wilding said he'd be here in time for breakfast."

"Yes. To everything. I'm starved." She reached out and gave the older woman's hand a squeeze. "Is your father all right?"

"He is, thank you."

"Great. I'll be out in a bit."

Just as she closed the door, Jack came out of the bathroom, wearing jeans that were zipped, but not buttoned. Too bad Mrs. Slattery had arrived before Lily had a chance to thoroughly explore every cut on that six-pack again.

"Think she was fooled?" he asked with a wry smile.

Lily bent to retrieve some underwear from the floor. "Save me a little dignity, okay? I don't want her thinking I fall into bed with perfect strangers on a regular basis."

"Do you?"

At the serious tone, she looked up. "No, Jack. I don't. Do you?"

"Once in a while." His half-hooded look told her that was the absolute truth. "But we're not strangers anymore."

"No, we're not. And I hope you'll do me a favor and

keep that aspect of our relationship secret in front of Reggie when he gets here today."

"Here?" He blinked at her. "Today? He's coming?"

"Of course." She folded her bra and panties into a tiny pile, deciding to carry them upstairs and get back to the room intended for her.

"Why?"

She frowned at him. "He wanted to get things started, I guess. Formally introduce us and explain what I can do for you."

"I think we handled the introductions just fine and…" His smile was lusty and sweet at the same time. "And you did a great job showing me what you can do."

She tucked the undergarments in her arms and lifted her chin toward the bed. "You know, Jack, I got a little carried away last night. Sex wasn't supposed to be part of the deal. That just…happened."

He looked at her for a moment, with humor and a little bit of question in his eyes. "I usually like sex to be part of the deal," he said. "But that's just me."

"Well, it's not going to be part of the deal for me."

He stepped back. "Okay," he said softly. "It's entirely up to you. Although we might get bored walking the beach and watching TV the whole time we're here."

"We won't be bored," she promised. "I have a lot on the agenda. We'll have to shop, have several salon appointments, and I like to do at least three meals in a restaurant to—"

"So I get to be dragged to boutiques, beauty shops and buffets, but no sex?" He tsked and shook his head. "That doesn't seem like a fair deal. I mean, it *just happened* last night—couldn't it *just happen* tonight?"

She'd never encountered this with a client in the two years she'd been in the business. "Maybe, when we're finished."

He frowned at her. "What? Like breakup sex?"

"Look, Jack, it's my business. But sleeping with you doesn't exactly scream 'propriety' now, does it?"

"It is your business, but…" He closed the space between them with a few long strides. "You want to know *my* personal motto about propriety, Lily?" he asked with a playful smile.

"Let me guess. We don't need no stinkin' propriety?"

He laughed. "Close. I usually say *screw propriety*." Which is why he would not be the poster boy for corporate image improvement. "But if you want to shop instead of bop, knock yourself out. I'll be down at the beach."

Did he think she could dress him for success without actually walking into a store? "I can't possibly do that without you."

Dismay darkened his eyes to a bottle green. "You can't?"

Of course, most men cringed at the idea of clothes shopping. And some men absolutely found it abhorrent.

"It can be fun," she assured him. "As long as you let me do what I do, and I promise, when we're done, you'll like the changes in you."

His eyebrows knotted and he took one step back. "You won't be the first to try and fail, you know."

"Reggie believes in me and I'm pragmatic," she said. "I see real long-term potential if we're successful."

"I better watch you," he said with a wary smile. "You are…relentless."

"I am," she agreed, wiggling out of his grasp. "But don't worry. It won't hurt too much."

He shook his head, his look taking that long, slow journey over her body again. "We'll take it one day at a time, okay?"

"That works for me." She stepped toward the door. "And don't worry about the coffee. Mrs. S. is taking care of me. Have a nice run. I'll see you when Reggie gets here for breakfast."

He tapped two fingers over his eyebrow in a mock salute. "Yes, ma'am."

"You keep up that attitude and this could really end up to be a pleasurable experience, Jack." She opened the door and gave a surreptitious glance down the hallway.

"Good. I like pleasure."

She blew him a kiss and whispered, "I noticed."

Jack didn't slow his pace until he'd finished the sixth mile and found his way back to the road that meandered to Reggie's house. Since Lily had let him off the hook for getting coffee in town, he'd chosen to run the rugged southern shore of the island, along the more aggressive surf of the Atlantic Ocean as opposed to the calmer waters of Nantucket Sound to the north.

He'd sucked in the salty, rain-washed air, reveled in the September sunshine and pounded sand until sweat stung his eyes.

And still he couldn't shake the feeling that something wasn't quite right.

And that didn't make a damn bit of sense. He'd met an extraordinary woman, had fantasy-quality sex with her and could look forward to at least two more days—or nights— of her company. So she wanted to shop and spa a bit. That was cool. In the evenings he knew what would *just happen*.

He slowed his step, pulled his T-shirt up to wipe his face and squinted up the hill to see the gabled manor silhouetted against the powder-puff clouds. And Reggie's Beemer parked in the circular drive.

That's what wasn't right. If Reggie wanted him to meet this woman and see if they hit it off, fantastic. And he hadn't said anything because he knew Jack would've balked at the idea, yeah, that made sense. Then why would Reg feel the need to fly all the way here from Manhattan and intrude?

He took a deep breath and bent over, putting his hands on his knees to stretch his back before standing straight again.

She never had said what she did for a living, she'd been vague about how she knew Reggie and she'd never even mentioned where she lived, for God's sake. Come to think of it, he knew basically nothing about her except her name.

And her sexual style. Which he'd classify as excellent.

Shaking his head, he stabbed his fingers through his hair and ambled up to the gate. *Just go with it, Jack.* What was wrong with him?

Entering through the back kitchen door, he was greeted by the smiling face of Dorothea Slattery, who looked up from the cooktop in the center island.

"Hey there, Dots." He grinned at her and watched the flush his secret name always produced. "What up, baby?"

"Hello, Mr. Jack." She gave him a fairly thorough inspection, probably not thrilled with all that perspiration in her kitchen. Or maybe the old meddler hadn't missed the fact that his bed had remained made all night.

"How's your pop doin'?" he asked.

"He's fine. His power was only out for a few hours. But

I didn't want to leave in case I had to go back in the middle of the night."

"We managed," he said with wink. "Left a mess for you in here, though."

She waved it off. "I'm just sorry that Mr. Wilding doesn't have a generator. I've told him and told him, but he's always so busy."

He leaned a hip against the counter and watched her sauté some onions, the tangy aroma rising to the copper hood that hung above the cooktop. "Tell me those puppies are going in an omelet with my name on it."

She beamed at him. "With just a hint of Swiss cheese and chopped tomatoes and thyme from my garden?"

"I love you, Dots."

Her cheeks nearly purpled. "This particular omelet is for Miss Harper. She's having breakfast in the dining room with Mr. Wilding right now, but if you take a shower before you sit on those white silk chairs of Mrs. Wilding's, I'll make one for you."

"Do I have to?"

"Yes."

He blew out a disgusted breath. "Just what we need around here. More women telling me what to do."

"You'll want to clean up for the meeting, Mr. Jack."

"The meeting?" He scowled at her and reached over to steal a piping-hot onion strip from the pan. Opening his mouth like a trained dolphin, he slurped it in. "You're kidding, right? What's on the agenda? The second date?"

She broke an egg into the pan. "Surely I don't know the advertising business, Mr. Jack. But Mr. Wilding referred to a meeting that would take most of the day, with Miss Harper."

What the hell was going on here?

"'Scuse me for a sec, Dots." He pivoted from the countertop and headed straight for the dining room, hearing Lily's laugh as he entered the narrow butler's pantry. Just like the first time, the husky sound of it sent a little frisson of sexual tension through him.

For a split second he was tempted to stop and listen. What was she saying about him? That she liked him? Yeah, well, he'd pretty much sealed that deal with her fourth orgasm. He barreled straight through the short hall and walked into the dining room.

"What's this BS about a meeting?"

Reggie looked up from the head of his mile-long rosewood table, his brown eyes popping behind rimless glasses. "There you are!"

Next to him, Lily sat with her back stick straight, her slender shoulders square, her gorgeous black hair pulled into some kind of updo and her hands folded on her lap.

The picture of...*propriety.*

He looked from Lily to Reggie and back to Lily. She lifted her chin at a Mona Lisa-like angle and gave him a cool nod.

What the...? He swiped the T-shirt over his face again, exposing his whole bare stomach to her while he did so.

"Sorry about the sweat, Reg," he said to the older man. "I just ran six miles."

"No sweat," Reggie said, then flashed his high-beam smile at Lily. "See why I'm in advertising?"

Jack didn't laugh, but scratched his cheek and studied Lily again. Finally, with makeup and styled hair, he could see her dry. She looked...dry.

"Good morning, Miss Harper," he said with exaggerated formality and a hint of a bow. "And how did you sleep last night?"

Only the quirk in her lips gave her away. "Good morning, Jackson."

Jackson? What was up with *that?*

He took a step farther into the room and lifted his chin toward Reggie. "I just heard there's a meeting and I wanted to know what it's about."

"Well, it's about you, Jack. And the agency."

A vine of uneasiness wrapped around his gut as he regarded Reggie's serious expression.

"The agency?" What the hell would Lily have to do with him and Wild Marketing?

With a silent apology to his favorite housekeeper, he pulled out a chair next to Lily and dropped onto the swan-white cushion. "Looks like the lights are on, but I'm still in the dark."

Lily took her napkin off her lap and pushed her chair back. "Why don't you two have a private discussion first and—"

Jack grabbed her wrist as she placed the napkin next to her plate. "Whoa, whoa, whoa. Stay right here, please."

She looked at him, a silent plea deepening almond-shaped eyes to sapphire. She needn't worry. He wasn't about to kiss and tell. But something—just as he'd suspected for the past hour—*something* wasn't right. "I have a feeling you know more than you're telling, sweetheart."

She looked apologetically at Reggie. "I must have misunderstood. Jack gave me the impression he knew this element of our business."

Their business? He raked her with a look, taking in the formal blouse, buttoned well over that cleavage he'd gotten so friendly with last night. Who described a hookup as *their business?*

A woman who wore that shirt, that's who.

Reggie's normally stone-smooth forehead bore more creases than Jack had seen in a while, and they were deepening with each passing minute. And behind those signature glasses his merry eyes looked…weary.

"Jack, I wanted to tell you this last night. That's why I had you come in early, and I absolutely planned to be here to launch this program and talk to you about our success strategy."

Launch this program? Success strategy? Why was his close friend, boss and personal mentor giving him a bucket of clientspeak?

"Shoot straight, Reg. This is me."

Reggie leaned back and tunneled his hands through his thick, almost totally gray hair, letting out a deep sigh. He looked every one of his fifty-six years, and then some.

"All right, Jack. Here's the deal. I've decided to sell the agency."

Jack just stared at him, and blinked twice. "You're selling Wild Marketing?"

Reggie nodded. "I have a very good reason."

Suddenly a sickening awareness took hold and he glared at Lily. "To her? You're selling it to her?"

For the first time, Reggie laughed heartily. "No, no. Is that what you thought?"

"I don't know what I thought." He seared Lily with a look. But whatever he'd thought, this had nothing to do with a setup for potential romance. Why hadn't she told him the truth? Why had she led him on?

"Lily is part of the deal, though, Jack," Reggie continued. "There's a slight catch with the contract and I think she can help us around it."

This time Jack sat back in his seat with a slump of surrender. "I think you better start from the beginning, Reg, because I am the victim of a serious misunderstanding."

Lily shook her head and held his gaze. "No, Jack. I misunderstood you. When you said you knew why I was here, I thought, well, that you did."

"Why *are* you here?"

Lily looked at Reggie, obviously waiting for him to explain.

"Jack, the company buying Wild Marketing is Anderson, Sturgeon and Noble."

"A bunch of uptight pri—jerks with broomsticks up their rear ends." He shot a glance at Lily, who didn't react. "Not that I don't like them or anything." Then the impact of what Reggie had said hit him. "They're buying Wild? That London firm? Seriously?"

"They're based in London, but they have offices around the globe. Their portfolio of clients is world-class and—"

Jack cut him off with a dismissive wave. "Can the copy, Reg. I know who they are. Why? Why would you sell Wild Marketing? To anybody?"

Reggie folded his arms and leaned on the table. "I can't refuse this offer."

Disappointment coiled through him. Reggie was the smartest brain in advertising, a gifted marketer, unparalleled in the ability to schmooze clients and harness the power of an imagination.

"Why would you sell?" Jack asked again, hoping for a

different answer, because the possibility of it being about money squeezed the life out of his chest.

"I have my reasons, Jack. And you…you would understand."

"Good. Tell me what they are."

Reggie closed his mouth and glanced at his hands, a gesture Jack had seen a thousand times when the man wanted to buy time and think of the perfect, processed response. But Jack deserved better than that. He waited.

When Reggie's eyes finally met his, Jack could read the message. *Trust me.* "I have a compelling reason."

But his blood had kicked into a slow boil and he'd long forgotten the woman next to him. Jack had come into Wild Marketing ten years ago, and in that decade he and Reggie had bonded into an incredible team and built Wild into one of the premier boutique agencies in Manhattan. Why would he let their rare and special little firm be swallowed up by some international conglomerate who wouldn't know kick-ass creative from…from an infomercial? No. No.

He shook his head. *Compelling reason* wasn't enough.

"You know that Anderson, Sturgeon and Noble will be the end of Jack Locke and your firm." Jack kept his voice modulated, with no need to slam the table while he issued the ultimatum.

"I knew you would initially react that way. But I've made special arrangements in the contract. The only way they can buy Wild Marketing is if you are named president and the head of their New York operations." He gave Jack an expectant look. As if he would jump up and down at the idea of being the president of Anderson, Sturgeon and

Ignoble? "And that's why Lily is here," Reggie finished, indicating with his hand that it was her turn to talk.

She sat a little straighter and trained her gaze on Jack. "My company is called The Change Agency," she said. "Reggie has hired me to work with you on a complete professional and personal image makeover to prepare you for the office of president and the management role that will require."

For a moment he actually thought his veins would burst when his blood hit two hundred centigrade. He opened his mouth, but nothing came out. No words. No jokes. No sound.

"It involves an external makeover and some performance coaching," she added. "I've developed a technique and have had success with—"

Anger whipped through him and he whacked his fist so hard on the rosewood that the coffee cups rattled. Lily's eyes widened, but she didn't flinch.

"—a number of individuals," she finished. As they stared at each other, she added, "I told you it wouldn't have to be painful."

He glared at her, then at Reggie, corralling a temper he didn't even know he had.

"No, thanks," he said quietly. "I don't need any coaching on my performance." He leaned over to Lily and gutted her with a look that he hoped reached right into her soul. "Surely you figured that out last night."

Her cheeks paled slightly, but again, no flicker of emotion in her eyes. Oh. She was a tough one, this Lily Harper. This agent of change.

Slowly he stood. "Best of luck with this, Reg."

"Jack, I need you."

Jack froze at the note of…what was it? Desperation?

Something in Reggie's voice that had never, ever been there before.

"I have to leave the business," Reggie said softly.

He had to leave the business? Jack just narrowed his eyes at his friend, his blood still heated enough not to trust what might come out of his mouth.

"The takeover by Anderson is contingent on having a president in place who knows the business and clients, because if we don't, we'll lose those clients and that business, and the new owners know that." Reggie's words were rushed, his voice as tight as the band that constricted Jack's chest.

"Then I hope you can find someone, Reg. But it won't be me in the navy-blue suit flying over to London for P&L meetings. Wrong guy. Wrong suit." He angled his head toward Lily. "Wrong approach altogether."

He left the room and hadn't made it halfway up the center stairs before Reggie reached him. "Wait."

He froze on the step and turned. "I'm leaving, Reg. I don't know why you're doing what you're doing or why you needed to butter me up with some sex kitten first, but I'm leaving."

Reggie took the few steps between them, putting his hand on Jack's arm. "Listen to me." Again Jack saw signs of pain he'd never seen before on Reggie's face: a clenched jaw and the down-turned mouth. "Samantha is dying."

For the second time that day Jack thought he'd been punched. "What?"

"She has inoperable brain cancer." Reg's dark eyes welled behind the glasses and Jack could hardly swallow. "I have to give her the one thing I haven't given her for twenty-five years while I chased my dream and my clients and my success."

Jack still stared at him.

"I want to give her time, Jack. Every minute I can, I want to be with her."

"Are you sure?" This couldn't be. Not the gentle woman who had never said a mean thing in her life, who only wanted children, and never had any. "Have you gotten a second opinion? A third?"

A spark lit Reggie's eyes. "That's the other thing I can give her. There is some chance, some possible surgery, but the cost is astronomical and the doctors are in Europe."

"You have the money, Reg." He gestured around the gargantuan hall. "Sell this."

He nodded. "I do. But if it works, I want to fund the program that can bring this surgery to the U.S. If it doesn't work, I want to give millions to research. Millions—" he tightened his grip on Jack's arm "—that I'll make by selling Wild Marketing."

How many slugs could a man take in one day?

"But Anderson wants a seasoned team member at the helm, Jack. They want the man who has been with me for the last ten years. The one who, we both know, built the reputation of our firm with the best damn creative mind in the business."

Jack held his gaze. "But they want him with a crew cut and wingtips."

Reggie smiled. "It's not that bad. I only want you to work with her to…polish up a bit. Just to impress them. She's amazing, Jack. You should see what she can do with a person."

"I have."

Reggie raised an eyebrow. "Buttered you up, huh?"

Jack managed a tight smile. "I'm sorry. I don't want to do this."

"Not even for Samantha?"

"Below the belt, dude."

"Do this for me," Reggie urged. "Work with Lily Harper, impress the guys at Anderson, keep the job for one year and then you're free to do whatever the heck you want and I'll back you." Once again he squeezed Jack's arm with a touch of desperation. "I'll back you. Please. Help me out."

Lily appeared in the archway that led to the dining room. Even with her uptight hair and right-wing clothes, she was beautiful. Her blue eyes locked on his, rich with challenge.

Aw, man. How the hell did this happen to him?

It didn't matter how it happened. Because she could cut his hair and put socks on his feet and teach him how to eat with the right fork, but she couldn't *change* him.

"How long does your average renovation take, Lil?"

Her lips tipped up. "A week at the most."

"All right, then," he said, melting her with one long look. "Let's do it."

And they would. Every single night.

Four

Lily stood silent for a moment as Jack disappeared into the upstairs hall, then she met Reggie's gaze.

"So," he said, his smile humorless, "that went well."

She met him at the bottom of the stairs. "I'm very sorry about your wife, Reggie. I didn't realize your desire to sell the company was so personal, or so painful."

"It is both," he acknowledged. "But I'm also sorry that Jack's not quite as amenable to my plan as I'd hoped."

"I think the tricky part will be getting him to conform without feeling like he's selling out."

Reggie sighed, pausing to remove his glasses and rub the bridge of his nose. "Have you ever had to work with someone who didn't want your services, Lily?"

She glanced at the steps, still seeing the challenge and

resentment in Jack's eyes. And something else. Fear? Anger? Tenacity?

She was no stranger to any of those powerful emotions. "Most people have hired me because they really wanted to improve their image, so they weren't reluctant. Still, he knows this is important to you and the business you've built."

"I have to get this deal made," he said, emphasizing that by putting a hand on her shoulder and squeezing gently. "And they won't accept Jack at the helm of the New York operation as he is. Without him, the sale will fall through, because the agency clients will follow him wherever he goes, and without clients, as you know, the business is nothing."

"I can polish him to a nice corporate shine, Reggie," she assured him. "Can you stay for a few days to help nudge him along a little?"

"I'm sorry, Lily. I have to get back to Samantha. Every minute is precious."

"I understand."

"Will you say goodbye to Jack for me?" he asked, cocking his head toward the stairs. "He generally only sulks for a few minutes."

She smiled. "I will." In one way, it was better to be left alone with Jack. She'd probably feel more comfortable with the process and the inevitable arguments. On the other hand, without Reggie, she was much more vulnerable to Jack's charm and the sizzling sexual attraction between them.

Well, the sizzling sexual attraction of last night. He surely wasn't interested in her anymore.

Reggie gathered a jacket from where he'd left it hanging on a post in the hall. "You know, Lily, I chose you for this job because I sensed an inner strength and a certain level of control that I thought a performance coach for Jack would have to have."

She nodded and murmured thanks.

"But don't you give up that control," he added.

"I won't," she promised, meaning it completely. "He's not that persuasive." Unless the lights are out and nobody's home, that was.

Reggie chuckled. "Yes, he is. But let me throw this into the mix before I leave."

She looked at him expectantly. Was he about to warn her out of Jack's bed? Had he assumed—correctly—that the *buttering up* Jack had referred to included sex?

"If you succeed at this job, there's a bonus in it for you."

Not at all what she'd expected him to say. "It's okay, Reggie. The money we agreed upon is more than fair."

"This isn't about money, not directly. This is about business. If you successfully make Jack into a textbook executive who impresses the British enough to get them to buy my firm, then I am willing to guarantee you the exclusive business for the entire firm of Anderson, Sturgeon and Noble. And I happen to know they are in the market for a professional performance coach to train the top executives in every one of their twenty-six worldwide offices."

She felt her jaw loosen. *Twenty-six worldwide offices?* All of the top executives?

"I would love that opportunity, Reggie." She almost laughed at the understatement. She couldn't even imagine having that much work, that much income, that much security.

He adjusted the jacket over his shoulders and nodded. "And I'd love to give it to you. But this job won't be easy.

It won't be a matter of changing Jack on the surface. You're going to have to make him think and act like a different man or the Brits will see right through it. So you, Lily, have your hands full." He gave her a tight smile and opened the front door. "I'll be in touch. Mrs. Slattery has been instructed to meet your every need. I'm counting on you."

"I won't let you down," she promised, reaching out to shake the hand he offered.

"Good luck, Lily." He started down the front steps to where his car was parked in the circular drive, then paused and turned back to her. "And by the way," he said, pointing a friendly finger of warning at her. "He's an advertising genius. He'll use anything he can to convince you he's right and you're wrong." He shot up one meaningful black brow. "*Any*thing."

"I appreciate the advice," she said, stepping out into the autumn sun in case his unambiguous comments sent a little heat to her face. He raised one hand in farewell and trotted to his car while she watched, thinking about the conversation.

She had so much to lose, and *everything* to gain with this project. She truly did appreciate Reggie's warning, but she wouldn't be foolish enough to let Jack derail her with sex. What they'd shared last night had been fantastic, but not worth the success of this makeover.

This was her chance. After all the years of classes, of service jobs, of night courses, of striving for something better her whole life. She'd never blow a chance to be the exclusive performance coach for a firm the size of Anderson, Sturgeon and Noble. She'd never blow the chance at the security she craved so much she could taste it.

Turning, she ran smack into a bare, broad, muscular chest.

Jack lifted one corner of his mouth, his green gaze relentless and penetrating. "Now it's just you, me and the housekeeper," he said. "You know what that means, don't you?"

She shook her head, a number of possibilities running through her brain. "What does it mean?"

"That you're outnumbered by people who like me just the way I am."

"Oh, I don't know, Jack," she said. "I think Mrs. Slattery would like you even with shoes on." She pointed to his feet. "We'll start down there and work our way up, okay?"

He rocked back on those bare heels, easily drawing her attention to the fact that once again he hadn't bothered to snap his jeans closed. "You know something, Lil? For a minute this morning I thought the shopping you had in mind was ring shopping."

She rolled her eyes. "Nope. Clothes shopping. For you."

"I thought you were looking for a husband."

"A husband?" She put one finger on his bare chest. "I don't need no stinkin' husband."

"Then we're even, Miss Manners." He grabbed her hand and flattened her fingers against his chest. "'Cause I don't need no stinkin' makeover."

She didn't move her hand, but let her palm absorb the feel of every hair, every inch of hot skin. "Too bad. You're getting one. Meet me in the library in five minutes so we can go over the agenda."

"We'll work down at the beach," he corrected.

And so the power struggle began. "No can do. I need my laptop to go over the agenda and walk you through the program." She tried to ease out of his grip, but he held her hand.

"Walk me through the waves. That library is too constrictive for me."

"It's September. The water's like ice."

"We can stay warm. And wet."

The tone, as much as the fact that she felt his pulse jump under her hand, shot a volt of desire through her and reminded her of Reggie's parting words. Jack would use anything to persuade and distract her.

"The library," she repeated. "With a shirt on."

"Okay to the library." He pushed her palm down an inch over a few coarse hairs. "But no to the shirt."

"This isn't tug-of-war, Jack," she said. He held her hand flat and firm against his chest, slowly forcing her palm over stomach muscles so well-defined she could count them. One, dip, two, dip, three, dip.

He stopped at the open snap. "Maybe it's just plain war."

She slid one finger behind the snap and placed her thumb on the other side. "I'll meet you in the library." With one squeeze, she snapped the jeans closed. "Wear whatever you want."

As she brushed past him into the house, she thought she heard him *tsk*. Or was that the jeans…unsnapping again?

"I have a plan."

Lily looked up from where she'd stationed herself behind Reggie's gigantic mahogany desk, managing not to blow out a breath of relief and victory at the fact that he wore a shirt. A tight black T-shirt with some red scratch of a logo across the chest, but still. Score one for Miss Manners. Two, if she counted the fact that she'd resisted the invitation to go swimming with him.

"Actually," she said, tipping the screen of her laptop so he didn't pounce on her agenda before she was ready, "I'm the one with a plan."

"My plan's better," he promised, setting a cup of steaming coffee on the desk in front of her like a peace offering. Then he sauntered over to a long leather couch against the wall across from her. "God, I hate this room."

He threw a pillow against the armrest and lay down, putting his bare feet up and balancing an insulated travel cup on his stomach.

"What's wrong with this room?" she asked, glancing around at the steep walls of books, the dark wood and few well-chosen prints. "It's got a very masculine feel, and it's full of wonderful books."

He closed his eyes. "It has too many walls."

"I count four. The usual number."

"You should see my loft in SoHo," he said, sitting up to take a sip of whatever was in his cup. "Two walls in the whole place. The rest all windows looking out over New York. Every room open, no blinds, no barriers."

"And no privacy."

"I turn the lights out when I want privacy," he said, balancing the drink on his solar plexus. "And I function well in the dark. Remember?"

As if she could forget. "Two walls and all glass, huh? Well, that tells me you're a man who doesn't like limitations or obstacles."

He chuckled, his stomach muscles nearly toppling the drink.

"As if you needed to see my floor plan to figure that out," he said, crunching up for one more long drink.

Then he set the cup on the floor and shifted onto his side, propping his head up under one hand. The position accentuated the length of him, and spilled a lock of golden hair over one eye. He looked like the poster boy for illicit sofa sex.

"So, Miss Manners," he said, somehow making the snarky nickname sound provocative. "Why don't you show me your plans and I'll show you mine?"

She tipped her laptop screen open and cleared her throat. "All right." She looked at the screen for a second, then back at him. She couldn't help it. He looked so much better than her PowerPoint slide. "I have devised a five-step program specially designed for top-level managers and executives. Would you like to hear it?"

"More than life itself."

"It includes work in each of the following areas—appearance, social protocols, body language, verbal and non-verbal communication skills and organizational skills."

"Let me see if I get this straight," he said. "We shop for some ties and hit a barbershop for a trim—that should cover appearance. Then we can have dinner at a restaurant with multiple forks to choose from to manage social protocols. A game of telephone should cover verbal and non-verbal communications. Which leaves organizational skills. How about I fold your clothes after taking them off you?" He grinned victoriously. "Good plan, huh?"

"You forgot body language."

He winked. "Like hell I did. That comes after the clothes are off."

"Jack," she said, situating herself straighter so that Reggie's oversize rolling, reclining desk chair didn't swallow her up and make her appear ineffectual, "it's a little more complicated and intense than that. Following a complete external makeover, I also help clients through an exercise of self-discovery. Knowing who you are, under-standing your flaws, weaknesses and points of vulnera-bility will help us create a way for you to handle—"

"Don't waste your time. I know my downsides." He absently twirled the cup on the floor, looking at her through that fallen strand of hair. "My flaw is that I like to sleep late, my weakness is chocolate and my point of vul-nerability? Sweetheart, you found that with your tongue around three-thirty this morning."

Heat burned. She knew exactly what spot he was talking about. Right below… "I'm referring to issues that impact your professional life and how you conduct your business."

"I conduct my business however the hell I want to." He shifted onto his back, to the classic "shrink's couch" position. Was he aware of that?

"After that," she continued, purposely not responding to his comment, "we'll put it all together for a final exam."

He turned to look at her. "Here's something for your self-discovery. I'm a creative guy and I hate tests. If it hadn't been for a baseball scholarship I didn't deserve I wouldn't have gotten in the second-rate college I did."

She heard the tiniest note of defensiveness in his voice and it nearly folded her in half. God, she knew that feeling.

"This will be a positive experience, Jack, I promise. I know you're reluctant to participate, that you don't want any part of changing or transforming or making any sort of professional renovation, but I believe you will benefit from this. And so will Reggie."

"This is a total waste of your time and my effort and

Reggie's money, but, hey. Whatever scratches your itch." He shrugged against the sofa. "Now you wanna hear what I have planned for you?"

"I'm the coach, Jack. You're the trainee."

His eyes twinkled with a silent *Yeah, right,* but he said, "How long are we trapped on the island here? Six days, five nights? Something like that?"

"We don't need to work at night," she said, clicking her screen to a mock schedule she'd made. "Anyway, if all goes well, you'll need some time off for good behavior."

Very slowly he pulled himself up and stood. "The time off *is* the good behavior," he said with a sly smile. "Ready for my plan?"

He came around to the side of the desk and parked one hip dangerously close to her, crossing his arms and looking down. She leaned back a little, the executive chair squeaking as it reclined an inch. "I'm not sure. Am I?"

"I'll be your own private science experiment for the daytime. Make me over, polish me up, change me into whatever the Brits want to see across the conference-room table. That's what you do, so you can do it all day long."

She looked warily at him. It couldn't be this easy. "What's the catch?"

He put his hands on the high back of the chair, tilting it enough to raise her feet off the ground. "At sunset…" He twirled the chair around in a dizzying three-sixty. "The tables turn."

She closed her fingers over the armrest and looked up at him. "How so?"

"You're in charge of the days…." He loomed above her, honey hair hanging over his chiseled features, his tight black T-shirt inches from her crisp white blouse, his long legs astride hers. He dipped the chair back until she was parallel with the floor. "I'm in charge of the nights."

"What exactly does that mean?" She dug to her own personal China to keep her voice steady, and barely succeeded.

"Whatever you do to me during the day, I get to do to you at night."

"I have to think about it."

"Think about this." He closed the space and kissed her, tilting her head so far back she swore the top of the chair almost hit the floor as his tongue slid between her lips and invaded her mouth. Blood rushed to her head, thumping wildly in her ears, and she did the only thing she could do— she grabbed his shoulders, hung on and kissed him back.

His lips were cold and creamy. They tasted like... Chocolate milk. Icy, rich, sweet milk. She curled her tongue around his and took another taste.

"So, Lil." He barely took his mouth off hers to speak. "Deal or no deal?"

"Jack, I—"

"Say deal and I promise," he said, softly cutting her off by flicking his tongue over her lower lip, "that I will do your whole stupid program from shopping to shoes."

"It's appearance and social protocol, not shopping and shoes."

"Call it whatever you want, baby. I'll still prove to you that you can't change me." He nibbled her chin and trailed a cool tongue over her jaw. "You have the days and I have the nights."

She hesitated, closing her eyes to try to think. But who

could think with all this man and testosterone and persua-
sion pushing her upside down?

"Come on, Lily. What do you have to lose?"

Her sanity. Her client. Her mind. "My balance."

"That's the fun part." He tipped her the last little inch,
forcing her hips right into his. "Deal or no deal?"

She could feel the power of him, the heat and sexuality
that rolled off him in waves, his hair tickling her face, his
muscles clenched against her body as he held her suspended, upside down, inside out. She could feel his daunt-
ing erection, growing steadily against her. It all made her
dizzy and crazy and wild and helpless.

"Deal."

She closed her eyes, expecting the kiss to seal it.
Wanting the kiss. Needing the kiss.

But he straightened the chair and backed away, leaving
her suddenly cold and seriously frustrated.

"All right, then, let's go shopping for my new wardrobe."

She blinked at him. "Shopping?"

"Appearance is up first, right?"

"Yes, it is." She smoothed her skirt, which had ridden
up her thighs as he tilted her back. "We'll start with a new
wardrobe for you."

"And one for you to wear tonight." He cocked his head
toward the door. "Meet me in the kitchen in five minutes.
I'll drive."

What in God's name had she just agreed to?

Five

Jack snagged the Jeep keys from the wall hook in the kitchen, not even considering taking the Mercedes two-seater that Reggie kept in the garage. He was more of a red Wrangler with the top down and the music up kind of guy, anyway. Especially on a killer Indian-summer day in Nantucket, a pretty woman by his side and nothing to do but…shop.

All except for the last part, he liked the way the afternoon was shaping up. He'd had enough time to think and come up with a strategy of his own. He wouldn't wreck Reggie's plans. He'd do what had to be done, especially for Samantha. If Reggie had to sell Wild Marketing, well, hey, that sucked, but Jack wouldn't stand in his way. Then he'd convince the suits in England that he was fine precisely the way he was, or he'd help them find a replacement.

Anything else made zero sense, and obviously Reggie

wasn't thinking straight when he proposed something as stupid as a corporate image makeover for Jackson Locke.

So Jack would simply take advantage of the time he'd been handed in a beautiful home with a hot, willing woman. He wouldn't do anything to jeopardize Reggie's chances of helping Sam, a lady he loved and admired so much that he flat-out refused to think about the possibility of her dying.

Jack would play Lily Harper's game. And then she'd play his. And when all was said and done, she'd like his game better.

He glanced around the kitchen, which sparkled with the handiwork of its keeper.

"Dots?" he called out. "We're going into town for a while."

The familiar gray head appeared from around the laundry-room door, a fluffy white towel midfold in her arms. "Taking the Jeep, Mr. Jack?"

He loved it that she knew him so well. "Yeah. You need anything in town?"

"No, thank you." She gave the towel a good snap. "I'm supposed to be getting what *you* need, Mr. Jack, and I was just trying to decide if I should make quahog chowder for you, or maybe you are interested in some of that fresh cod I steamed up for you last time you were here. I can do whatever you like, Mr. Jack."

"Better than anyone," he agreed. "Make the chowder and I will have to marry you, Dots."

She laughed. "If I were forty years younger and thirty pounds lighter, I would do just that."

Lily came into the kitchen, a bag on her shoulder and a light jacket thrown over one arm. She'd changed from the uptight suit to linen trousers and a pullover. She looked good, all Nantucket upscale casual, but still not as good as she had soaking wet climbing out of the bathtub.

"You would what, Mrs. Slattery?" she asked.

"I would be delighted to make both the cod and chowder for dinner tonight."

"I'm sure that would be lovely," Lily said. "But I had something more formal in mind. Can you recommend the best restaurant in town?"

Mrs. S.'s face fell in disappointment. "You're standing in it, but if you insist on going out, I suppose you could try the Sconset Café. Maybe a bit pricey, and it's not necessary to go wrestling with the leaf-peepin' tourists when I can make you anything on that menu."

"Better," Jack added.

But Lily powered on. "I need something with linen tablecloths and lots and lots of silverware."

"Because," Jack interjected again, "we'd just slurp chowder and eat cod with our fingers if we stay here."

Lily shot him a look, but Dots stepped out of the laundry room, a question in her eyes. "Whatever would you need all that silverware for?"

"I'm getting etiquette lessons," Jack said, opening the fridge to grab water. "Apparently Lily and Reggie think I need an extreme makeover." He shook some strands of hair out of his face. "And a haircut."

"A haircut!" Mrs. Slattery's eyes flew open in horror. "Your hair is perfect!"

He just chuckled and shrugged. "Gotta give the woman her props, Lil. She calls it like she sees it."

Lily remained unfazed, slipping into her jacket with her

lips pursed. "All we want to do is make a few minor adjustments, Mrs. Slattery, to get Jack ready for his role as an ad agency president."

"Do they have to have short hair?" she asked.

"They have to have a certain look. And," Lily added, "they are expected to follow certain social protocols and codes of behavior. All we're going to do is give him a few lessons. Nothing that will mar his *perfection*."

She couldn't have doused the word in any more cynicism if she'd tried. He resisted the urge to remind her she'd thought he was pretty damn perfect when he nibbled her into nirvana the night before.

"Well, keep your hands out of his hair," Mrs. S. mumbled, heading back into the laundry room.

"Hey hey hey, Dots. Don't go crazy." Jack winked at Lily. "She can put her hands in my hair if she wants. It's the scissors we want her to avoid."

The older woman paused at the door and looked from one to the other, her expression morphing from distrust to love as her gaze landed on Jack. "You won't be able to get into any of the nicer places without a jacket and tie, Mr. Jack," she warned. "So perhaps—"

"He'll have several jackets and ties very soon," Lily assured her.

He spun the key ring around his index finger. "The fun never stops. Let's go, Miss Manners. Dots, you can try a reservation at Topper's, but we may not get in on a Saturday night. If not, then book something for tomorrow, and we'll have cod and chowder tonight."

She beamed. "I've already picked the fresh thyme from my garden for you."

He blew her a kiss, then swept an arm toward the back door. "Miss Harper, your chariot awaits. Hope you don't mind four-wheel drive and a roll bar."

Lily followed him outside to the detached garage, where she paused to admire the SLR McLaren Reggie kept stored for special occasions.

"Wow." She reached toward the car, but seemed unwilling to actually touch it.

"Yeah, that's what four hundred thousand dollars will getchya." He barely glanced at the car, but heard the bit of wonder in Lily's sharp gasp.

"It costs that much?"

"I think Reggie stole it for three eighty-five. It's the closest thing to a baby he and Sam will ever have." At the thought of Sam his throat closed, so he ripped the rag top off with a little more force than necessary and crammed it into the back of the Jeep, along with thoughts of losing Reggie's wife.

"Now, *this* baby purrs." He patted the side of the Jeep lovingly as he held the door open for her. "You'll see. We'll take the scenic route to town,"

"Every route is scenic in Nantucket," she said, settling into the Jeep and reaching for the seat belt.

"The colors in September are good, but October would blow your mind."

Her gaze lingered lovingly on the Mercedes. "That car blows my mind."

He threw her a surprised look as he shoved the key into the Jeep's ignition. "I wouldn't have taken you for such a status seeker, Lil." He reached down and lifted her bag to check out the logo. "Not Fendi or Kate Spade, I see."

"Not yet," she said softly, and the tone yanked his attention.

"So is that what this is all about? A quest for the holy dollar?"

She didn't answer while he pulled the car out and maneuvered around the long, circular drive.

"I don't think there's anything wrong with wanting the finer things in life," she finally said as he pulled up to the intersection of Hammock Pond Road and shifted gears to hold the car on the hill. "Don't tell me you wouldn't enjoy having a car like that if you could."

He could. But she didn't need to know that. "Look at that view," he said, looking straight out at the hills dotted with weathered gray buildings, the trees tipped in russet and topaz, the white-capped navy water of Nantucket Sound in the distance. "That's what I call one of the *finer* things in life. Who cares if you see it from a Jeep or a Benz? The view's the same." He threw the car into gear and barreled out onto the highway. "But knowing your motivations makes this easier."

He could practically feel her bristle next to him. "My motivations aren't the issue."

"Still, it's good to know what fuels your soul." Once he had the car in fourth, he dropped his hand onto his own leg with a thud of disappointment. Lily Harper was in the game for the gold. What a shame.

"Money doesn't fuel my soul," she said defensively. "But I appreciate nice things and the comfort and freedom that a good income can bring. Is that morally reprehensible?"

He shot her a look and laughed. "Hey, I wrote the book

on morally reprehensible. No, wanting cash is not evil. But greed is."

"Greed?" She turned in her seat to face him. "There's nothing greedy about making a living. About wanting security and comfort. And if there's a nice car and decent wardrobe in the mix, that's not bad."

He'd hit a hot button, and filed the place where she kept it hidden in case he wanted to tap it again later.

"So how does one become a performance coach?" he asked after a moment. If she appreciated the change of topic, she showed it only by shifting forward and looking straight ahead. "Did you go to special training or do you make it up as you go along?"

"I've had various kinds of training," she said, her voice vague as she looked out the window. "But it's interesting how you phrased that. Do you make things up as you go along? Is that your corporate style?"

He laughed softly. "If I had a corporate style, you wouldn't be here. And of course I make things up. I'm the creative director. That's the definition of my job."

"How did you get into advertising?"

"The same way I get anywhere—through the back door. I can sketch. I can write. It was the only business that I thought might accept a nonconformist." He closed his eyes for a second. "*Was* being the operative word."

"You don't have to conform," she said quickly. "Just follow the rules and guidelines. Is that so hard?"

He dropped his hand from the gearshift to cover her thigh, feeling the tensed muscle under the fabric of her pants. "Rules and me, we're not such good friends."

She made no move to slip out of his touch. "Think of it

as a game, Jack. You like games. You let them think you fit the mold, and the sale goes through and everybody's happy, but you are still doing the work your clients hire you to do."

"You make it all sound so simple and sensible."

"That's *my* job," she said. "And remember, you're doing this for a good cause."

He threw her a sideways look, catching the way the wind pulled some strands of dark hair out of the twist she had it in, whipping them across her face. One got caught in her lip gloss and he reached over to tug the hair that stuck to her moist lower lip. "Believe me, if the cause wasn't good, I'd turn this thing around and we'd spend the weekend in a whole different direction."

"Let me guess. Horizontal?"

He shrugged. "Or standing up on the widow's walk on top of the house, watching the sunset over the ocean. Or maybe here in the old Jeep, right back there." He pointed his thumb over her shoulder and saw her fight a smile. "Then again, there's always the sailboat Reggie has down at the harbor, so we could do it bouncing on the water."

"Oh, I've never been sailing before."

"Good, we'll go over to Cape Cod later this week."

"Cape Cod? Could we make it there and back in one day?"

He shrugged and narrowed his eyes. "It's about four hours over, even against the wind. But we can stay at my sister's in Rockingham. Assuming she's not in the hospital having a baby."

"She's pregnant?"

He nodded. "Yep. Having a girl. You want kids, Lil?"

If the change of subject threw her, she didn't flinch. "I'm pretty busy keeping myself afloat to think about kids."

Translate that into too busy climbing the corporate ladder in order to make big bucks. "That's cool."

"And you?"

Unlike her, he wouldn't bother with a euphemism like "I haven't met the right person" or "Someday." He just told the truth. "I like to get up and go whenever I please. Kids and a wife would probably cut into that."

He turned the Jeep onto the main road of Nantucket's precious town, eyeing the rows of brick and whitewashed clapboard, and the packed narrow road. As he slowed down, an SUV pulled out about twenty feet in front of him, leaving a nice big vacancy.

He grinned at her. "The parking gods love me."

"Great. How about the shopping gods?"

"I don't call on them too often. But there's the Toggery," he said, indicating the only upscale men's store he knew on Nantucket. "Of course, I've never been in there, but I believe that building houses enough suits and ties to make your conservative little heart go all aflutter."

She turned to him, beaming. "Perfect. And thank you for being so agreeable to this."

"I'm not agreeable. Believe me, I have an ulterior motive."

"What's that?" she asked, climbing out of the car.

"I heard they have nice big dressing rooms." He winked. "So you can, you know, help *change* me."

She laughed, but he could tell she wasn't sure if he was serious or not.

Lily loved the store the minute she entered it, loved the rich smell of good fabric, the comfort of natural hardwood under her feet, the low-key attitude of the staff and even the soft jazz music in the background. She could dress Jackson Locke very nicely in here.

She glanced at the changing rooms and noticed they were small and not very private. Relief quietly battled disappointment. Not that he would really...oh, yes he would.

She launched into a full attack on the racks and stacks, assessing quality, cuts and sizes with a shrewd eye while Jack followed along, throwing out the occasional quip and gripe. But for the most part, he cooperated.

"You like this, don't you?" he asked as she chose and discarded garments to match the vision she had in her head of an ad agency president.

"I used to be a professional shopper," she said absently, narrowing her eyes at the collar of a shirt, then glancing at him before deciding against it.

"*Used* to be?" He stayed close to her as she moved down a line of suits, touching the fabric, frowning at colors.

"For *other* people," she corrected, almost laughing at the idea that she could afford to shop like this for herself. Someday, but not yet. "That was my job, as a personal shopper."

"Is that how you put yourself through college?"

There was no way to stop the automatic response of heat to her face. Her clients were all college educated, all from white-collar backgrounds and fine families. While she... wasn't. And regardless of the fact that she was doing everything to change that, some shames, she knew so well, never really die.

"No," she said, turning to hold the pale blue shirt up to him, high enough to cover her face. "This might be good for you."

He lowered the shirt. "So where'd you go to school?"

"I didn't. Nope. Too much purple in that blue. Clashes with your eyes."

He rolled the very eyes that clashed and followed her to the next shirt. "Where do you live, Lil?"

"Outside Boston."

"Boston? Did you grow up there?"

More heat rushed to her face. "Around the area."

"You don't have the slightest Boston accent."

She chose another shirt and handed it to him. "Here. I've worked on getting rid of it."

He set it back down. "No tab collars. Why did you want to get rid of a New England accent?"

Because it sounded so poor and blue-collar. "It's better for my job to have what you call a 'TV accent.' None at all."

"And how did you go from personal shopper to executive image consultant?"

They were off her childhood, and she felt safer. "Well, it just sort of evolved," she said, moving to a rack of ties and holding the suit jackets out. "I've always liked to watch and observe people, and I took some corporate transformation workshops and read a lot of books and I decided to launch the business." She turned to him, narrowing her eyes. "The dressing room's over there. Here." She handed him a stack of clothes and urged him in the other direction. "Get started, Jackson."

"You don't want to undress me?"

More than anything. "Just change and let me see how that looks on you."

A few minutes later she heard him clear his throat as he stepped out of the dressing room. She turned from tie racks she was browsing, and almost gave in to a full body shudder, lifting a fist to her mouth with a soft "Oh."

A three-thousand-dollar suit fit as though the designer had custom-made it for him. The dark jacket hung open, the crisp white shirt was unbuttoned at the collar and his feet, of course, were bare.

Even with the flop of long hair hiding one eye and that sneaky half smile, the suit transformed him from bad-boy sexy to big-boy powerful.

"Wow," she whispered. "Whoever said clothes make the man was—"

"Naked." Stepping around her, he padded barefoot to a three-way mirror and looked at each angle for less than a nanosecond. "Yep. Fine." He turned away from the image. "We done now?"

"Stop," she said, grabbing two neckties and heading straight toward him. "You really need to relax and enjoy the experience."

"That's what my dentist says."

She held up one tie to his chest, then the other. "Yellow is conservative," she said, switching them again. "But, oh, there's something about this pink. You don't have issues with pink, do you?"

"I have issues with ties." He took one and twisted it around her wrist. "Unless there's a headboard and some knots involved."

Wordlessly, but unable to keep the smile from her face, she reached up to slide the pink one around his neck.

"Because," she said as she buttoned the collar. "It says a lot about a man who is confident enough to wear a pink tie."

"It says you're an idiot for wearing a noose." He slid two

fingers behind the button and pretended to choke. "Why would anyone put one of these things on? What purpose can it possibly serve?"

"Besides their original utilitarian purpose of hiding buttons and finishing the look of the suit, the right tie sends a message of control and power and impacts how others perceive you and your ego."

He tugged again, nearly wrecking her perfect half Windsor knot. "What you mean is the bigger the tie, the bigger the thing it points to?"

She patiently continued the knot. "Sexuality is part of your overall aura, yes." She patted his chest and stepped back to look at him. "That works very nicely," she said, turning him around so he was facing the mirror again. "Look at you. You'll wow them in London."

"I'd rather wow them with a good TV spot for their top client," he muttered as he started to shimmy out of the jacket. "That's what they should care about. Bag it up and let's get out of here. I have somewhere else I want to go."

She pulled the jacket back over his shoulders. "We're not done. You need more suits. Several shirts. A few ties. And shoes."

"I have shoes. I wore them here."

"You need a complete wardrobe, Jack, and you wore five-year-old docksiders here."

"Six." He managed to get the jacket off and fling it onto a nearby chair, and he had the tie loose around his neck in one fast move as he returned to the dressing room.

Two minutes later he emerged back in jeans, the black T-shirt and the half-dozen-year-old docksiders. He dumped the stack of clothes into her arms. "I wear a size twelve shoe. I trust your judgment on style, although please no wingtips. I'll see you when the sun goes down."

She fought to keep her jaw from dropping. "Where are you going?"

"Somewhere I can breathe." He placed the car keys on top of the pile of clothes she held. "I'll get myself home. We've met your agenda for today—new wardrobe. If I spend one more minute in here, I'll do something crazy. Trust me, Lil. You don't want to see that."

Before she could respond, he was out the door, leaving her with an armful of clothes and a heart full of certainty that Jack Locke was one man that no woman could ever really have and hold. And for some reason, that made her chest ache.

Six

Jack tapped once on Lily's bedroom door, then eased it open. "You dressed, Miss Manners?"

"Yes."

"Too bad."

She stood at the dresser, wearing cotton pants and a pastel sweater, brushing out her long hair.

"You were right," she told him. "We couldn't get into that restaurant."

She set the brush down and turned around with a silky-smooth toss of long black hair. The sweater dipped to a sweet V neck and narrowed at a tiny waist. Sexy, classy and so completely wrong for what he had in mind.

"I have a better option," he assured her.

"Where have you been all day?" she asked.

He pulled a very large tissue-topped shopping bag

from behind his back. "Picking up some things you'll need tonight."

Eyeing the bag, she squinted at the Ladybird logo. She'd seen the store that afternoon…and had been tempted to enter. "Lingerie?"

He shrugged. "What else would you expect from me?"

She scooped up a jacket and her handbag from the bed. "I thought doing the unexpected was your secret weapon. Didn't you tell me that?"

He didn't set the bag down, but let her pass and walked with her to the stairs.

"So what do you have in mind tonight?" she asked, a sneaky smile on her face as she glanced at the bag.

"The unexpected."

She didn't respond to that, and as they walked to the car, he talked about Cape Cod, telling her about the small town where he grew up, in Rockingham, where his sister still lived, married to his best friend from high school. She asked questions about his parents, now retired in Florida, but, he noticed, she provided only vague answers when he tried to ask about her own childhood. Not for the first time, he suspected Lily Harper had some secrets.

"You know what I like best about Nantucket?" he asked as they turned onto a winding road, heading toward the wilder, less populated southeastern hills of the island.

"God, everything." She inhaled a deep breath of the crisp autumn air that wrapped around them. "Look at that view of the ocean."

Beyond them, the Atlantic Ocean darkened as night fell, deepening the golds and russets of the trees and taking the sky from plum to navy with each passing minute.

peninsula, not much more than a dirt mound and a few small trees surrounded by a sea of floating cranberries.

When he cut the motor, the silence was total.

"This, Lily," he said with a reverence he felt down to his bones, "is life without walls."

Her gaze moved from east to west, taking in nature's watercolor. "It's beautiful," she finally said. "I've never seen anything so ethereal, so spooky and stunning at the same time."

He smiled, satisfied that she got the appeal of one of his secret places. The click of insects, the whisper of leaves and an owl's hoot echoing over the bog were the only sounds. Except their slow, steady breaths.

"You know what's interesting about a cranberry bog at this time of year, right before the harvest?" he asked. "The underwater bridges."

She gave him a quizzical frown. "What are they?"

"Well," he said, turning to grab the bag he'd shown her earlier. "The water is between two and six feet deep, with a gazillion cranberries floating along the top."

"Yeah?"

"And in order to harvest without a boat, which not all the workers used to have, you have to climb in and find the underwater bridges and walkways. Which is what we're about to do."

She drew back. "We are?"

He held the bag toward her. "Here you go."

"You want me to wear lingerie into the bog?"

He chuckled. "Just a bag, sweetheart. The only one I could find to carry hip waders and steel-toed shoes."

"Excuse me?"

"Come on, Lil. It's moonlight, it's sweet fruit, it's scary and adventurous and…" He leaned across the console to whisper in her ear. "It's my turn to introduce you to some new things."

She choked softly. "Walking through cranberry bogs?"

"Wading," he corrected. "I told you I like the unexpected." He pulled out the waders he'd folded in the bottom of the bag. "You thought I had a camisole and a thong in here, didn't you?" He tsked, shaking his head. "What a cliché that would be."

"With you, I never know what to think."

He grinned. "Aw, Lil. You couldn't have paid me a higher compliment."

Two hours later Lily was still laughing. This time when they drove away, however, Jack opted for headlights, which he'd disdainfully referred to as "the chicken-shit way out of the bog."

They provided enough light for her to see the red stain that covered her hands, the only skin that had touched the actual bog, thanks to his thoughtful delivery of hip waders and his obvious skill at finding underwater bridges.

They hadn't fallen in once…but they'd come close. She'd clung to him for security and his hearty laugh had echoed over the moving, waterlogged fruit farm. He'd never stolen so much as a kiss out in the fog and water, a move that might have been designed to make her comfortable, but only made her realize how much she wanted to kiss him, and taste the sweet fruit on his mouth.

"How do you know so much about cranberries, anyway?" she asked.

"I told you, I was raised in Cape Cod. I love the bogs, so I worked harvests after school from the time I was fifteen for extra money."

Was it possible he knew what it was like to have no money? "Money for what?" she asked.

"The usual. Gas in my Camaro so I could take pretty girls on dates." He glanced at her. "Why the look? You jealous?"

Maybe of the fact that he'd had a car. *Gas in my Camaro* was a far cry from food stamps and money to buy shoes from the thrift store. "Nah," she assured him.

"My buddy Deuce and I used to pay way too much for Red Sox tickets, and it wasn't cheap getting to and from Fenway Park."

She plucked at some cranberry twigs stuck in her hair. "You were baseball fans," she said absently. Not poor. Not penniless. Just *normal*.

"Deuce was way more than a fan. He played pro ball for the Las Vegas Snake Eyes until last year. But then the impossible happened and now he's a coach at Rockingham High and bracing for that baby girl due in two weeks."

"The impossible? Wait, he's married to your sister, right?"

"Yep. Proving that the love gods are capable of the most unlikely miracles."

"What do you mean?"

Jack shrugged. "They belong together, Kendra and Deuce, but they had a past so dark, I never thought either one could see the light. Then the gods, and Deuce's father, intervened. Ready to see my real favorite spot in Nantucket?"

He whipped onto another side road and started a steep climb up.

"Sure. Where is it?"

"The top of the world, baby." He put his hand on her leg. "And Dots packed our dinner in that cooler back there and I threw in a blanket. No walls, just right." He patted her leg. "Tomorrow. I promise tables, napkins, forks aplenty. Tonight I vote for high on a hill, overlooking the sea and the bog, under a blanket."

"You mean on top of a blanket."

"My bad."

She chuckled and shook her head. "Why not? This is already the strangest date I've ever been on."

"Do you date a lot?" he asked.

"No. I work a lot."

"A workaholic, huh?"

"Not really." She looked up at the stars, wondering how much to tell him. "I work, like most people, to make enough money to live."

"What's enough?"

She sighed. "Above the poverty line, below the Forbes 100 list."

"I don't work for the money," he said. "That's why I'm having a hard time getting my arms around this whole thing with selling the agency."

"But you understand why Reggie needs to do it."

"Yeah." But he was quiet as they wended their way up the hill. "We're almost dead center on the island now. From up here, you can see Hyannis and Martha's Vineyard and on a clear day you can see whales in the Atlantic Ocean. And if you look to the southwest, you can see the bog we just waded."

When he parked, she climbed out and did a full turn, taking it all in. "Wow. This is incredible. Who owns this land?"

"Some dude with more money than time," he said with a wry chuckle. "But he doesn't care if we come up here."

He spread the blanket, lit a tiny portable lantern and started emptying the contents of a cooler while she circled the top of the hill and studied the lights of Cape Cod thirty miles away.

"I forgot silverware."

She just laughed. "Why am I not surprised?"

"C'mere, Lil." He patted the blanket and held out a thermos. "I told you we'd drink the chowder and eat the cod with our fingers."

"You called it." She joined him, a shiver running through her that had nothing to do with the early-autumn air.

"We don't need no stinkin' silverware." They said it at exactly the same time, with the same intonation, punctuating their harmony with a laugh.

She took the open thermos and held it to her mouth. "Here goes."

"Fear not, Miss Manners. No one's watching but me."

And he was watching intently, studying her face, leaning close enough to almost touch her.

She took a sip, letting the hot, rich, velvety soup fill her mouth. "Mmmm." She swallowed and automatically reached for a napkin, but he wiped the corner of her mouth with his fingertip, then licked the drop of chowder.

Taking his own sip from the thermos, he added, "Dots is the one woman I might marry. She loves me unconditionally and she makes a mean quahog chowder."

"Those are your requirements for marriage?" she asked, waiting for her turn to share more delicious soup.

"I have no requirements for marriage because I don't believe in it."

"You don't believe in it? Or you don't believe in it for you?"

"Both. What does that piece of paper mean? It's a paper wall, that's all, easy to tear down and throw away. There's something about mating for life that seems so... confining."

She looked at him, the moonlight catching the angles of his strong face, the shadow of his unshaved jaw. "And yet humans do it all the time," she said, hoping the whisper of sadness in her heart didn't come out in her voice. "Even walls of paper can be lasting if they're built with enough love."

"Very ideal thinking, Lil. And I say, hey, if that's what you want, go get it." He opened a container to reveal crispy fried cod. "And you, I suspect, are a woman who gets what she wants."

What she wanted was to change the subject from marriage to work. It was far more comfortable. "What gives you that impression? How I shop?"

"Nope." He broke off a piece of cod and reached for her mouth, sliding it between her lips without even waiting for permission. "How you make love."

Leave it to Jack Locke to avoid a comfortable topic. "How's that?" she asked when she managed to swallow the bite.

"You take what you want, when you want it, how you want it."

She held the thermos and looked hard at him. "Did you think I was selfish last night?"

"On the contrary. You were bold. Confident. Aggressive. All seriously attractive qualities, I might add."

"In bed, at least."

"In life, too. Here." He held the cod to her mouth. "Let me feed you."

For a moment she just looked at him, then she opened her mouth and he slipped another piece of cod between her teeth. It tasted fresh, like the sea itself.

"This is the best way to eat, don't you think?" he asked, giving her another bite. "Outside, under the stars, sharing bites."

"You do manage to make everyday activities more…" *Sexy.* "Interesting."

He gave her the tiniest smile. "Another perfect compliment, Lil. Thank you."

With that thought and those words hovering around them, she let him feed her the rest in silence, pausing to admire the lights of Cape Cod and the whitecaps dancing on the ocean.

When they finished, he opened a bottle of water for them to share, and he dropped back on the blanket to look at the stars while she sat next to him. When she leaned back on her hands, he curled a finger into the ends of her hair, twirling it as though it were the most natural thing in the world, sending sharp twists of desire through her with every casual touch.

"You're a master of seduction, Jackson Locke," she said, turning to glance down at him.

"I'm not going to seduce you," he said softly. "I just want to know your secret."

"My secret?" Her heart kicked a little, and not just because of the way he looked flat on his back, his hair falling to the sides. "My secret to success?"

"No."

She looked at him again. "My secret weapon?"

He tugged gently at a lock of her hair. "Your secret. I know you have one."

She cleared her throat, since swallowing had suddenly become impossible. "Everyone has secrets, Jack. Let's see...I read the funny pages first. Does that count as a secret?"

He propped himself up on one elbow and feathered her hair some more. "I mean the secret you are trying so hard to hide."

"I don't know what you're talking about."

"Don't lie to me, Lily. There's something about your past that makes you evasive. You have a secret. And tonight you're going to tell me what it is. Now, as a matter of fact. Before we leave this hillside."

All she could do was stare at him.

Because when she opened her mouth, the truth was going to come out and she was going to tell him the one and only thing she'd never admitted to anyone.

And that, she realized with a wallop of her heart, was his *real* secret weapon.

Seven

For one quick second Lily considered using sex to get him off the subject.

Instead, she took the bottle from his hands and sipped some water. "I don't know what you mean by a secret."

"Whatever you call what you're hiding. A past. The truth. The real you. Lay it on me, Lil."

"I'm not hiding anything." Her look and tone were a little too tight, a little too harsh. But how did he *know?*

He sat up and moved his hand to her nape, his fingers gently burrowing into her hair to send a waterfall of chills down her body. "Then why did you blush when I asked where you went to school?"

"Because I didn't graduate from college, and some people, some clients especially, think that's a strike against me."

He laughed softly. "You really think I'd care about something as conventional as college? Me?"

"Well, you're different. No one's like you."

His fingers curled as he stroked her neck. "You're killing me with these compliments. But why are you so vague about your childhood?"

She moved away from his touch, hugging her knees to her chest. "Because my childhood is not the issue here. This week is about you, about your makeover. You are the one on a voyage of self-discovery, not me."

He snorted softly. "I don't need—"

"No stinkin' self-discovery."

"Amen to that, sweetheart. But you do."

Blowing out a breath, she glared at him. "No, I don't."

"Hey," he said softly, leaning his whole body into hers. "You agreed. You do what you want to me during the day and I do what I want to you during the night."

"I thought that meant sex."

"Tonight it means finding out your secrets."

She stiffened next to him, and she knew he felt it. How could he not? "I'd prefer sex," she said, her voice as low and dark as her heart.

"We'll get to that." He slid his arm around her, gently inching her closer. "Tell me."

There was no way he was pulling this out of her. No. *Way.*

Maybe no way. Maybe…

God, if anyone in the whole world would be sympathetic and understanding, it was Jack Locke.

Suddenly, unbelievably, she wanted to tell him. *Everything.*

"I am not really hiding anything. I'm just a little embarrassed about my…" She expected him to fill in the blank, but he didn't. "My humble beginnings."

"Your parents were poor."

"My parents?" The word stuck in her throat as she looked at him. "My dad disappeared when I was two. My mom raised me alone and we weren't poor. I believe the word is…"

"Destitute."

She bit her lip, took a breath and looked him straight in the eyes. "The word is homeless."

He didn't move. Didn't draw back in horror or pity or shock.

"In fact," she continued, fighting a lump the size of a Ping-Pong ball in her throat, "I know firsthand the unique disgrace of living in a car, a shelter and, one particularly bad year, a toolshed."

Almost imperceptibly his arm tightened. "How long did you live like that?" he asked.

She ratcheted up her chin, held his gaze. "The longest time? A year. Eventually, when I was about eleven, we finally got a small studio apartment in Waltham and my mother got jobs cleaning houses for rich people." She shrugged. "Maybe you wouldn't consider them rich, but they seemed like millionaires to me. She died when I was seventeen."

"No wonder you want money."

"No, I want security. I want to never live like that again. But I learned a lot."

"About living on the streets?"

She smiled. "No. About rich people. Before my mother died, and after, I spent lots of time in those people's houses, when I wasn't in school. I watched them. I helped set tables for dinner parties. I talked to the help. I observed how they lived, what they wore, how they talked. Then, when I went out on my own, I tried to emulate them."

"You obviously learned well," he said, tightening his hold on her. "Because you dress, talk and look as classy and well-bred as any woman I've ever met."

Her shoulders, which she hadn't realized she'd held square and stiff, dropped with a sigh. "Thank you."

"Lily." He stroked her cheek with the lightest touch of his fingertips. "You should be proud, not ashamed."

Yeah, right. "Well, I coach a lot of people who obviously lived well and went to college. I couldn't. In fact, I had to quit high school at sixteen so I could work. I was a waitress and a hairdresser, and then I got a job at Bloomie's as a personal shopper." She didn't wait for his comment, but powered on, as though a dam had broken and she wanted to overflow with the truth. "I took some night courses, but I always had to work to make ends meet, so I've been working and working. This opportunity, this chance to get international clients for my little agency, well, Jack, this is the chance of a lifetime."

Now he did draw back a little. "No wonder it's so important to you."

"Of course. I can finally, *finally*…" She gave him a tight smile. "I want to buy a house. That's all I want in the whole world. It's my dream, my burning, most powerful dream. I want to own a house. Nothing grand, nothing special, but I want to own it. Free and clear."

"Makes sense," he said.

"Of course it does. And not just because of my background. I think having a home, a real home, matters to everyone. But most people take it for granted."

"It doesn't matter to me," he replied. "Houses mean walls."

"Well, we're different that way, then. But this job is really important to me, Jack. Succeeding with you and proving myself to Reggie can mean the breakthrough I've wanted my whole life."

"I see." He nodded slowly. "Seems you and Reggie have pretty compelling reasons for wanting this deal, and this makeover, to go through."

"And you're sweet to go along with it." She brushed the single strand of burnished hair that fell over his eye. She loved that lock of hair. Loved to twirl it around her finger, as she did right then. "I've never told anyone that, you know. About my past, or about my dreams."

"Now, that—" he closed his fingers over her hand and brought it to his mouth, kissing her knuckles "—is the greatest compliment of all."

For several moments they said nothing. They sat close, while her heart continued at a gallop, her eyes still stung from unshed tears and her hand stayed securely in his.

She finally broke the silence. "Well, Jack, you got me to eat with my fingers, forgo a napkin and tell my darkest tale. You sure managed to wreck my first social protocol lesson."

He kissed her cheek. "Wait'll you see what I do for body language."

"I can't." She turned so that their mouths aligned. "Start now," she whispered, leaning close to kiss him.

His response was tender at first. But she deepened the kiss, offering herself, and when his hands slid over her sweater she moaned softly to let him know how much she wanted his touch.

In a moment he guided her onto the blanket, positioning his long, hard body on top of hers.

"We're going to make love again," she said, feathering his beautiful hair as it fell over his cheeks.

He stifled a little laugh as he pulled the sweater higher and lowered his head to tend to her breasts. "Looks that way."

"Even…after…you know about me."

Moonlight caught the glint of seriousness in his eyes when he looked at her. "You can't really think that would change how I feel about you."

"How do you feel about me?"

He rocked his hips against hers, as though his obvious arousal answered the question.

"I know how you feel about my body, Jack. I meant me. Me. A person who's been so poor she practically lived in a cardboard box."

He didn't even blink. "I told you walls hold no allure for me. You were a kid, Lily. A child who has obviously used the lousy hand dealt to you to build a productive, useful life and, in the process, help other people fix their own problems. It's amazing, really. And admirable." He half smiled. "At least, it would be if you weren't slathering those renovation talents on me, but since you are…" He rocked again. "And since we're here…" He kissed her cheek. "And since I happen to like the hell out of you…"

"Let's make love."

He laughed, a little bit of a growl, a little bit of a sigh, punctuated by a slow, wet kiss. "Yeah. Right now. Right here on this hill, under these stars. Let's make love."

He grew hard against her stomach and their hips began to rock in a timeless, natural rhythm. Heat shot between her legs, and she curled one calf around his knees as their kisses turned hotter and wetter and wild.

He touched her everywhere, stripping clothes, licking skin, tasting secret places, suckling her into a state of dizzy, crazy desire.

She tried to think about what this meant. That for the first time in her life she was going to make love with someone who knew the truth about her, who knew what she was made of and where she'd come from.

But she couldn't really think about anything.

Only the way he felt in her hand, pulsing with need to be inside her. Only the way her body opened to him, taking him willingly, so deep that he touched her womb with the first thrust. Only the way her teeth sank into his shoulder and he whispered her name as pleasure so exquisite it bordered on pain racked her body until she coiled around him, tighter and tighter and tighter.

She couldn't think of anything as she finally gave in to the quaking fury of an orgasm that started in the center of her body and rolled over her until every single cell was utterly and totally satisfied. A moment later he shuddered with his own release, just as ferocious and complete as hers.

And when he finished, she still couldn't think. All she could do was hold on to Jack, because she felt like she'd fall right off the edge of the earth if she let go.

As he had every morning for the past five days, Jack woke with the sun on his face, a woman in his arms and a hard-on that had become so commonplace, he could actually ignore it at times.

He shimmied against Lily's taut backside. This would *not* be one of those times. She responded by moving exactly as he'd hoped, sliding to the north so he could glide south into the hot, tight envelope of her womanhood.

Without breaking the silky, wet contact, he reached over his shoulder for the condom packet he knew he'd left unopened on the dresser. But before he grabbed it, Lily jerked around, stealing her warmth with a gasp.

"Tomorrow's our last day."

"In Nantucket. Not on earth." He handed her the foil wrapping. "Do that thing with your teeth, Lil."

She shook her head. "You have to get a haircut. Reggie could call any minute and that's the one thing we haven't done."

"I can pull it back into a ponytail."

She looked at him as if he'd suggested a pink-tipped Mohawk.

"Listen," he said, digging for reason in his voice when what his body was feeling was so far from reasonable. "I've endured your entire repertoire of professional performance coaching for five solid days. Thanks to you, I can delegate like the commander in chief, communicate with precision, conduct quality meetings, disarm verbal hostility and take the sting out of criticism. In addition, I know how to stand to project authority, which fork to use on my shrimp cocktail, and I can do a one-handed half Windsor knot in my sleep. I own a pair of cuff links, for cryin' out loud. You're *done*. Leave my hair alone."

She pushed one of the offending strands from his face. "That's good, Jack. You're getting so good at responding resourcefully to criticism."

He took her hand and placed it over his erection. "Criticize this."

"Oh." Her eyes widened and, like every time she touched him, her lips parted, her breath caught. "Nothing wrong with that."

He held the condom packet out to her. "Teeth. Open. Use. Now."

"Haircut. Salon. Ten o'clock. Today." She flipped over and rolled out of bed. "See? I can speak gorilla, too."

Narrowing his eyes, he dropped the packet on her empty pillow. If sex as a diversion didn't work, what would? "I'll get my hair cut tomorrow. Today we're going sailing."

She froze midway between the bed and the bathroom, turning around slowly. "Sailing?"

Her smile was so pretty, it damn near hurt to look at her. But the rest didn't make him feel much better, either, with all those feminine dips and curves, creamy white skin, a tiny dark tuft between her legs and nipples the color of juicy pink raspberries. Lily was so sexy and sweet and adorable, his whole insides twisted every time he studied her, with or without clothes.

"Later," he said, patting the bed with a hand that literally itched to touch her. "Come back now and let me love you, Lil."

He caught the nearly imperceptible flash in her eyes and tamped down a matching spark of guilt. He didn't mean *love* that way, of course. But they'd gotten so familiar, so affectionate, so much like lovers in the past week. The sting of her makeover was completely neutralized by the balm of sex that got more familiar and even more exciting every time. Sex that was so much fun, he didn't even want to think about this week ending. Especially if the grand finale included his hair on some swanky salon floor.

"Didn't you say it would take four hours?" she asked, still not approaching the bed.

He smoothed the sheets in invitation. "I can go four hours. Can you?"

"I meant to sail to Cape Cod. You said it would take four hours."

He leaned over to squint through the shutters and gauge the wind in the trees. "There's probably a light chop. If we get favorable winds and decent weather, yeah. We can leave by ten and be there by three at the latest."

"And we'd stay there overnight?"

"There's plenty of room. Deuce built a mansion on the beach." Again he saw the little flicker of something in her expression. Money. Mansions. Was that envy he saw, or fear that her childhood secret would be revealed? Or maybe she didn't want to go that next step and meet family? Maybe that was too much for her.

Funny, it wasn't too much for him. And it ought to be. He wanted her to meet Kendra, and he, man, he wanted Deuce to meet her.

"Do we have to stay there?" she asked.

"Why wouldn't we?" He propped his torso on one elbow. "Think of it as a test of your skills."

"My skills?"

"Your image consulting skills. If I've really changed, if you've succeeded in morphing me into the Donald Trump of advertising, then the two people in the world who can confirm that are my best friend and my sister. Let's go and take a test drive before we try and hoodwink the Brits."

"We're not going to hoodwink anyone. You *have* changed."

His gut roiled, but it was true. At least she'd helped him see how to blend authority and creativity. And he didn't hate the way he looked in her power suits—at least not when she took them off him…with her mouth.

"I haven't really changed." But even he could hear the uncertainty in his voice.

The Agent of Change had, to be fair, done her thang. At least on the surface.

Her navy eyes tapered. "Fine. We'll test you out at your sister's. Then tomorrow morning we go to Hair Apparent for a cut."

"A trim."

"A style."

He rolled his eyes. He had a day left. And a night. He'd think of some way out of it. Instead of arguing, he just shot off an irreverent salute, then waved the condom packet like a white flag. "Then will you do that trick with your teeth?"

"Of course I will." She turned, giving him one blissful view of her backside as she trotted off to the bathroom. "At least once more before I go back to Boston."

He fell back onto the pillow, the condom slipping from his hand. Why did the idea of that kick him in the stomach with the same intensity as the thought of seeing Ad Agency President on his business cards?

Business cards? He didn't even own them. Although he'd bet his next big idea that they were being printed right this very minute.

He exhaled and waited for the hard-on, and the headache, to subside.

He just didn't want her to leave, was all. That had happened to him before, hadn't it? He'd liked plenty of women over the years. He'd even grown fond enough of a few to date them for more than one phase of the moon.

But then the walls closed in and the demands grew louder and they wanted…an *arrangement*. They wanted structure and limitations and titles, like Mr. and Mrs. That's when he lost interest.

But with Lily, he had this bizarre sensation that he hadn't even hit stride on the interest level. He wanted more. More of her body. More of her laugh. More of her heart.

What was wrong with him? Had he forgotten that her idea of the perfect life matched his general depiction of *imprisonment?*

Falling for her, *caring* for her was just so dumb, it defied logic. The woman lived for security, for God's sake. For a house, permanence and stability. He knew that without a doubt because when they weren't busy having mind-blowing sex or doing mind-numbing professional coaching, they talked. Constantly.

Over food, along the beach, in the hot tub, at the kitchen counter at three in the morning where they devoured Dot's leftovers to build stamina for the next round. She had such a great appetite—for everything.

He knew what she wanted out of life. Just as she knew he needed freedom and a life without limits with the same urgency that he needed air, water and sex.

So why, then, did the idea of their interlude ending put a hole in his heart? She hadn't succeeded in making him over *that* much, had she?

He stabbed his fingers through his hair and snagged a

bunch of morning knots. Swearing softly, he untangled the mess.

This was crazy. He would *not* cut his hair. Any more than he would buy a house and live in it with the same woman...forever.

Some things could *never* change.

Eight

Lily's very first sail was just like everything else she did with Jack: exhilarating. Senses overloaded, she clung to the teakwood trim of Reggie's twenty-nine-foot sloop, the massive canvas popping with the wind that danced them over Nantucket Sound, a delicious bath of September sun warming her face, the heady smell of salt water and sea clearing every thought from her head.

The visual wasn't bad either: a brawny, long-haired Viking at the helm, wearing a loose, knit shirt and khaki pants, working the sails with the ease of a man born and raised near the water. His muscles strained as he cut the jib and raised the mainsail, generously sharing the new vocabulary with her and guiding her through the steps as they tacked and shifted into a steady, cool northern wind.

"Would be a lot easier with the wind at our back," she

shouted over a gust that tipped them perilously sideways, taking her stomach and equilibrium with it.

"The path of least resistance," he said through gritted teeth as he fought a gust, his hair snapped straight back, his eyes hidden by reflective shades, "bores me." He laughed with the sheer fun of it. "Coming about!"

She dipped low as the boom swung across the deck, rocking the boat as it cut into the new direction.

"Isn't she a beauty?" Jack asked, tapping the helm of the *Lady Sam* with affection. "Reggie doesn't take this thing out enough."

"Why not?"

"He's a workaholic. Even when he comes to Nantucket, he's either running a brainstorm or pitching a client or hauling a mountain of files."

"That's going to change," Lily said, not sure if Jack heard her soft comment in the breeze.

But she knew by the look on his face that he had. Before he responded, ocean spray splashed up the side of the boat, soaking his shoulders and hair. Jack shook his mane like a lion and hooted with delight.

Mesmerized, Lily watched him. He looked like a billboard for a man in the prime of his life, taking on the elements and winning, loving the challenge and laughing in the face of a cold wave of misfortune.

Something tightened in her chest, a foreign, scary and still lovely sensation of awe and wonder and terror.

Jackson Locke, with his disdain for barriers and his love of freedom, with his biting wit and clever mouth, with all his irreverence and talent and creativity and heart and raw, untamed sexuality, was the most attractive human being Lily had ever met.

That's what tightened in her chest, what had been damn near squeezing the life out of her for the past week. Love.

She could fall in love with him.

The boat rose and fell over a wave, slapping hard against the water and sending a jolt from her spine to her brain.

"Coming about!"

She could fall in love with him. Easily. In fact—

"Lily! Down!"

She blinked at the boom careening toward her so fast she didn't have time to think or gasp. She dived, missing a slam in the face by a millisecond and actually feeling the buzz of canvas right over her head. Embarrassed and stunned, she stayed bent over, her brain whirring and her blood pumping like the wind-whipped sheets overhead.

What was the matter with her? *Love* him? Of all the bad choices in the world, that one was without equal.

"Hey."

She didn't realize Jack had abandoned the helm, and was kneeling in front of her, his hands on her knees. "Are you okay?"

She managed to nod.

"You almost got creamed."

"I'm okay." But still she didn't lift her head. She couldn't look at him. He'd know. He'd read it in her eyes. He'd draw another secret from her, plucking truths like flowers from her heart.

"Are you sick, Lil?"

"I'm fine." Slowly she sat straight. "I just wasn't listening and…I'm fine."

He'd pushed his sunglasses back on his head, regarding her with an expert gaze that darted from eye to eye. "You look a little pale. You sure you're not seasick? 'Cause if you have to blow, just lean over the side."

She fought a laugh. "I don't have to blow, Jack."

"Then what's the matter?"

The matter? How about she'd just realized she was falling in love with the totally wrong man? A man who had no use for what she wanted, a man who should be issued with an expiration date on relationships? A man who...

"Nothing," she lied. "Really, it just surprised me. I'll be more careful."

He squeezed her legs and winked. "We can drop anchor and go below if it'll make you feel better."

"Sex isn't the answer to everything, Jack." The wind flipped some hair across his face and she did what she always did, instinctively. She brushed it back, letting her fingers slide through the silk and graze the morning stubble on his cheek, waiting for his inevitable joke about sex most definitely being the answer to whatever ailed her.

But he leaned closer to her face, almost kissing her. "You scared me, Lil. I thought I lost you there."

He would lose her, eventually. He would lose interest and move on to the next thrill, the next free-form relationship, the next challenge. She'd be nothing but the woman who tried to make him over. And failed.

The boat tipped to an angle and he shot up, righting it with a confident turn of the helm, then a quick look at her.

"You sure you're okay, sweetheart?"

Her stomach roiled with the next wave. She could hide

this from him. He didn't need to know she'd fallen so hard. He'd never get *this* secret out of her.

"I'm sure," she said, a practiced smile firmly in place. "I avoided disaster."

And she would again.

"All right," he called over another salt spray. "You ready? Coming about, Lil."

This time she ducked the swinging boom with ease, and used the opportunity to hide her face while she whispered the words she'd never, ever say to him. Just for the pure thrill of feeling them on her lips.

I love you, Jackson Locke.

"Now, that's what I call tall, dark and handsome."

Jack didn't even have to look up from the line he was tying to see who meandered across the wharf planks in their direction. Only one man he knew elicited that universal response from the female population.

"Yeah? I call him fast, wild and married to my sister."

"So that's Deuce Monroe."

"The one and only. I told him to meet us down here and drive us into Rockingham." Jack snapped the line into a tight cleat pitch and straightened to follow Lily's gaze. "Whoa, look at him."

"Okay. If I have to."

He threw her a dirty look. "I mean for a has-been pro ball player, he looks pretty damn…happy."

Deuce hustled toward them with his usual athletic grace, but there was something else in his step. Something about the way he held his broad shoulders and the beaming smile on his face.

When Deuce had returned to Rockingham two years earlier, kicked off the Las Vegas Snake Eyes baseball team because of a major league mistake, he certainly hadn't beamed or bounced. But all that had obviously changed, and Jack knew exactly who'd been responsible for the change.

His sister, Kendra.

Deuce's signature heartbreak smile widened as he approached the sailboat and hoisted himself on board in one smooth move.

"You must be Lily," he said, reaching out a hand to pull her up from the cushion and greet her at the same time. Another smooth move. "I'm Deuce, the brother-in-law."

It wasn't the phrase that surprised Jack; it was the bone-deep pride in Deuce's voice that caught his attention.

He was used to the fact that Kendra had married his best friend. Hell, she'd crushed on him since the time she could write her name. Even when he broke her heart and ruined her life, she never quite got over him. And then, a decade later, Deuce reappeared in Rockingham, and for a while there it looked as if history was going to repeat itself. But they'd worked it out, Kendra had forgiven Deuce the sins of his past and they'd been married for well over a year.

Lily returned the greeting with her own heartbreaking smile, then Deuce turned to Jack and they gave each other knuckles, then a masculine hug and friendly back pat.

"Good to see you, Jackson."

"You, too, dude. How's Kendra?"

"Glorious," Deuce said, that pride glistening in his eyes again. "She's going to be the most amazing mother. Of course she has everything organized and ready, every detail covered. She even—"

"So she feels okay? Everything with the baby is fine?"

"The baby's great. You can see her kick. It's so cool. And wait'll you see the nursery, man. We went a little nuts with pink."

Jack shot Lily a look. "I was worried about this. The aliens beat us here and took Deuce away." He frowned at Deuce. "Who *are* you?"

Deuce laughed. "The husband of your sister. The father of your niece. The coach of the old Rock High team."

But not the player—on the field and off—he used to be.

"You sound like a very happy, very excited, very proud papa," Lily said. "I'm looking forward to meeting your wife."

"Good, 'cause I don't like to leave her alone for long these days. Let's go."

Jack helped Lily onto the dock and she walked down the wharf, studying the boats and the weatherworn buildings at the port outside Rockingham. He knew enough about her social protocol to realize that she was giving him a moment alone with Deuce. Still, he took some of that moment just to admire her, and wonder what she'd think of his hometown. Then he stepped back onto the boat to grab the keys.

Deuce had scooped up a single duffel bag from the deck. "This it? You two sharing a suitcase?"

"And a room," Jack said pointedly.

Deuce lifted one eyebrow. "I thought this was a work arrangement. Isn't she supposed to be some kind of executive coach?"

"What can I say? The sex gods adore me. And so does she."

"You and your gods." Deuce rolled his eyes and shouldered the bag. "Don't you get tired of jumping from one bed to another?"

"Oh, like you were Mr. Celibacy when you were single."

"Maybe I wasn't. But now I'm Mr. Monogamy, and one of these days you'll see the light."

Jack made a fake punch at Deuce's shoulder. "I see the light has blinded you, dude. Which is a good thing, since you married my sister."

"Love has blinded me. Wait'll it happens to you."

"I can wait. Obviously, some clichés are true. Misery does love company."

With a hand on Jack's shoulder, Deuce nudged him around so they were facing each other. "Hey, pal. Do I look miserable?"

Why lie? "No."

Deuce notched his chin in Lily's direction. "She's nice."

"She's more than nice," Jack said, studying her right along with Deuce. "She's…she's…" He shook his head. The string of adjectives would embarrass him if he started to say exactly what Lily was.

"Whoa, this is a first. Words elude Jackson Locke. Film at eleven."

Jack pocketed the keys and climbed out of the boat. "Shut up, Monroe."

"And he has no funny comeback." Deuce dropped into his best color announcer's voice. "This could be serious, folks. This could mean the game is well and truly…over. Could it be we are a single strike from the end of a stellar career as one of Rockingham High's greatest players?"

Jack speared him with a warning look. "Would you can it?"

Deuce laughed, shouldering the duffel bag and following Jack out of the boat. "Wait'll Kendra finds out."

"Kendra finds out what?"

"That you're in love."

Jack opened his mouth to argue, then closed it again. Not because words eluded him. But because he didn't trust what he might say.

Kendra Monroe closed her eyes and, for the twentieth time that hour, rubbed her swollen belly with a deep inhale of satisfaction. Lily was sure it was twenty, because she'd counted every happy sigh, every maternal pat, every exchange of affection between the prospective mother and father. Joy permeated Deuce and Kendra's beautiful waterfront home. Joy and security and love and permanence.

Lily could practically taste the contentment in the air, as thick as the salt off Nantucket Sound just fifty picturesque feet from where the four of them finished dinner on the wide deck.

"That was wonderful, honey," Kendra said to her husband, patting her belly. "Jackie loves your barbecue chicken."

"Jackie?" Jack shot forward from his seat and blinked, incredulous. "You're naming the baby after me?"

"We're naming her after Jackie Mitchell," Deuce corrected. "One of the first professional female baseball players, who signed with the Chattanooga Lookouts in 1931."

Jack looked at Lily, unconvinced. "They're naming her after me."

"Your ego knows no bounds," Kendra said, chuckling

fondly at her brother. "I knew you'd think that, so I didn't tell you."

"I love that you're naming her after me," he continued, undaunted. "I'll be the best godfather in the world. The kid will want for nothing."

Lily reached for her water, hoping a sip would cover the impact his words had on her. He would, of course, do anything for his about-to-be-born niece. Jack would be a stellar uncle, one who would take the baby for wild shoulder rides and shower her with frivolous, expensive gifts and a lifetime of love.

Because there were no walls, no rules, no limitations with a niece. Not the way there would be with his own child. The thought twisted her heart and she sipped again.

"Don't you think, Lily?" Kendra asked. "I mean, you know Jack better than anyone now that you've been his professional coach."

Lily set the glass down slowly. What had they asked her? "I'm sorry…"

"She's sorry she won't reveal trade secrets by answering that," Jack said, shooting her a look that said he knew she'd lost track of the conversation. She'd like to take credit for teaching him that social skill, but she knew better. He was way too adept at reading her body language…and sometimes, she imagined, her thoughts.

"No, I won't," she said quickly with a smile of gratitude. "But, tell me, does the name mean you expect her to play baseball?"

Kendra laughed. "You obviously didn't get up to her room yet to see the unorthodox decorating scheme. Who knew you could get pink catcher-mitt-shaped pillows?"

"Come on," Deuce said, standing and grabbing an empty platter to take it into the kitchen. "I'll show you my masterpiece."

"This I gotta see," Jack said, also standing and picking up some dishes. "You coming, Lil?"

"I'll see it in a little while," she said, not exactly anxious to tour the nursery with Jack and hear any remarks about how Deuce was *trapped*.

Not that he'd made any so far, but she knew Jack. "I think I'll get a little more of the sunset with Kendra and then I'll clean up."

"Thanks, Lily," Kendra said. "Deuce won't allow me to lift a finger, as you've noticed."

Deuce leaned over his wife, holding the platter out while he dropped a kiss on her hair. "You are thirty-eight weeks pregnant, Ken-doll. You're not supposed to do anything but grow that baby."

She smiled up at him, and for the twenty-first time rubbed the basketball-shaped tummy. "We're fine, honey. Don't worry about either of your girls."

His expression said that he did, but he just dropped another kiss on her head and looked at Lily. "Holler if her water breaks."

Behind Deuce, Jack looked skyward. "Holler if my cell phone rings," he mocked.

When they left, Lily settled in to chat more with Kendra, who was a sweet and feisty feminine version of her older brother, although her eyes were blue and her hair much lighter than his.

It would have been easy to seethe with envy when faced with a woman like Kendra Monroe. She had it all—

love, marriage, a baby on the way and a house so warm and welcoming and safe that Lily literally ached when she walked into it.

But Lily didn't ache from envy or jealousy—she'd spent her whole life longing for what Kendra had, so the sensation was as natural as breathing. No, this hurt was different. This was new and scary. Now her ache had a face. A name. A body. A head of gorgeous hair, a heart of pure gold and a resistance to commitment that was so much a part of him, it was stamped into his DNA.

"I think you've done it, Lily." Kendra's statement pulled Lily from her thoughts again, but this time Lily wasn't about to act as though she knew what her hostess meant.

"I've done what?"

Kendra shifted on her chair, squinting into the last rays of sunlight bouncing off the water beyond the whitewashed clapboards of her home. "Well, for one thing, Jack put his napkin on his lap before we started eating and I could have sworn I noticed him switch forks between the salad and main course."

Lily smiled. "A small victory, but it should help the cause." They'd explained the entire situation to Deuce and Kendra over dinner, spelling out the reason Lily was there and why Jack had agreed to the idea of coaching.

"And," Kendra continued, "I can say since I'm his sister and lived with Jack for most of my life, I don't think I've ever heard him so adept at keeping a conversation with Deuce off baseball and high school, and on to things that the whole table cares about."

Lily nodded. "He was easy to guide in the area of social protocol."

"He'll make an excellent ad agency president, and, believe me, there was a time when I didn't think Jack would be anything but a starving artist."

"He'll fool the Brits, anyway," Lily conceded. "If I can get him to wear shoes and cut his hair."

Kendra shook her head and took a sip of water. "Good luck with that. The only time he kept it short was during the spring and summer baseball seasons, and only because Deuce wanted his best friend on his team and pleaded with him to follow the coach's rules."

"He hates rules," Lily said.

"With a passion," Kendra agreed. "Jack's just always been that way. Hates restrictions. Hates structure. Hates policies, guidelines and most systems of government."

"He hates walls, too," Lily said with a laugh.

Kendra leaned forward. "But he sure likes you."

The words kicked her gut. "Yes, well, we have…we get along…we are sort of…compatible."

"You are sort of crazy about each other is what you mean."

The idea that she and Jack had a relationship so open and obvious that his sister could see it made her heart dance. And then sink. "It was fun," she said quietly.

"*Was?*" Kendra's baby-blue eyes widened. "It's over already?"

"Well, as soon as he goes back to New York, I'll be going to Boston. And with luck, every one of the twenty-six cities where Anderson, Sturgeon and Noble has an office."

"So your paths will cross," Kendra said hopefully. "You'll see Jack. If you get the assignment, you'll be a consultant to his firm."

Lily had thought of that. A million times. "Yes, of

course. But…" They wanted such different things out of life that crossing paths would never be enough for Lily. Although it might suit Jack perfectly. "We'll see," she finished weakly. "It all depends on how well he pulls off the executive makeover."

Kendra looked across the table at her, one hand slowly rubbing again. "He'll never cut his hair," she predicted. "It would take an act of Congress, an act of God and more influence than even you can have to get him to do that."

"He has to. He promised. The whole thing is a waste of time if he walks into a meeting with the British owners with hair down to his shoulders."

Kendra shrugged. "Well, if you get him to cut his hair, then, honey, he must really love you."

The glass-top table suddenly vibrated with the hum of Jack's cell phone.

"Well, what do you know?" Kendra said with a sly smile. "My water didn't break, but his cell phone rang."

Lily picked up the device and peered at the caller ID. *Reggie Wilding. 911.*

"It's his boss," she said. "And it's important."

"Answer it," Kendra said. "He won't mind."

She was right. Jack wouldn't think she'd invaded his privacy—911 could mean anything. It could mean something happened to Samantha. Lily flipped the top open. "Hello?"

"Lily? Is that you?"

"What's the matter, Reggie?"

"Nothing. At least, I don't think so. Robert Anderson and Russell Sturgeon are coming to the office tomorrow. They want to meet Jack."

She fell back against her seat. "Tomorrow?"

"Is everything okay?" Reggie asked. "You haven't called in a few days. I thought perhaps things weren't going along as planned."

She thought of her revelation on the boat. Things were definitely *not* going along as planned. "What time tomorrow?"

"They'll be here at two o'clock. I need Jack on a plane early tomorrow morning. There's one more commuter flight out of Nantucket tonight, I think. In an hour or so. You'll have to hurry."

Oh, Lord. "We're not in Nantucket, Reggie. We sailed to Cape Cod."

"Cape Cod?" He practically choked.

"Don't worry." Although she was, she wouldn't let the client know that. "He can fly out of Boston first thing in the morning." Wearing…*what?* She looked across the table and held Kendra's gaze. Surely Deuce owned a nice suit.

Oh, she could just see it. Jack sauntering into the meeting in some ill-fitting suit, barefoot, his hair a wild, unholy mess from running through airports.

It didn't matter. She had to make it work. Jack had to make it work.

"Lily, I want him in this office tomorrow, dressed to impress and spit-shined to a blinding finish. They're bringing the contract and I intend to sign."

The sliding door opened behind Kendra as Jack and Deuce, laughing at something, came back to the patio.

"He'll be there." Lily flipped the phone closed and looked at Jack. "The British are coming. And you're expected to be in New York, in full battle gear, tomorrow. We could sail back now, get your stuff and try and get a morning flight to Manhattan from Nantucket."

"That's crazy," Deuce said. "I have plenty of suits."

Jack didn't speak, but he held Lily's gaze for a long time before asking, "Kendra, do you have any scissors?"

"I sure do, but are you planning to cut Deuce's suits to fit?"

"Nope. Lily's going to cut my hair."

Kendra lifted one very impressed eyebrow at Lily. "She is?"

"She is," he said with a quick wink. "It's showtime."

Nine

"I can't do it." Lily clunked the shears onto the marble vanity in the guest bathroom and Jack opened his eyes, catching her expression of dismay in the mirror.

"You can do it. You used to be a hairdresser. You told me."

"I didn't know you were listening."

"I listen to everything you say and some things you don't." At her narrowed eyes, he shrugged. "Hey, you're the one who spent a day teaching me how to read body language." When she didn't answer, he pivoted on the little vanity stool to face her. "You can do this, Lil."

She sucked in a deep breath, and shook her head on the exhale. "It's a crime. Your hair—it's…" She fingered it the way she always did, threading her index finger through a lock in the front, twirling it with affection. He loved that gesture.

"It's just hair."

"It's *you*." She slipped her hand deeper into the hair, palming his nape, raising his face to hers. "Maybe we could do something with a ponytail?"

"I think the aliens got you, too."

She smiled weakly. "A wig?"

"I'll do it myself." He reached for the scissors, but she grabbed them first.

"You can't cut your own hair."

"I can do anything."

That made her laugh softly. "Honestly, I can't believe we're having this discussion. It should be the other way round. You should be fighting me, I should be begging you."

"You'll beg later, when you get to pretend you're making love to Mr. Right…wing." He tapped her chin with a finger. "Hey. We can't quit now. Deuce loaded me up with some Armani pinstripes and your favorite—a pink tie. I can even squeeze into those slick black loafers of his. We're not going to back down now just because of a logistics glitch, are we?"

"You're right," she said. "And Kendra told me you used to cut your hair short so you could play on Deuce's baseball team in high school."

"You bet I did. And I made a ritual out of it."

"What did that entail?"

"I'd go down to this place on a beach just south of town and have a sacrifice to the hair gods."

She laughed, still shaking her head. "You're too much."

"I'm serious. I'd take my mom's scissors, two of my dad's beers—which I would chug before I cut because the hair gods demanded it or else your hair would never grow again. Then I'd take all the hair I cut, let it fly in the wind and wash the rest off butt naked in the water." His lifted an eyebrow. "And that was in March."

She snagged a washcloth from a basket and wrapped it around the scissors. "Go get the beer and let's go."

His jaw dropped as he grabbed her hand. "At midnight? You'd go to the beach and cut my hair?"

"Don't sit there and ask questions, Jack Locke. The hair gods are waiting."

But he had to sit there. He couldn't move. He was stupefied by…by her. By this perfect, irresistible, adventurous woman who totally *got it.*

"What are you waiting for?" She tried to tug out of his grasp.

"For this." He gave her a solid pull, landing her on his lap. Then he kissed her with every ounce of passion he could muster, hugging her into him and taking possession of her mouth the way she'd taken possession of his heart.

When the kiss ended, she opened her eyes and winked. "Now, don't forget the beer. We don't want to anger the hair gods."

His smile came from deep inside, from his chest, from his soul. But then it faded. How could he ever let her go?

Half an hour later he dragged a blanket and four of Deuce's best imported lagers out of the Monroes' brand-new family-friendly SUV to what Lily had dubbed "the sacred salon."

As he laid out the blanket, she popped a brew and did a little twirl to check out the deserted beachhead and the natural rock jetty that stuck like one long finger into the water, worn smooth from a few millennia of waves.

"So how long have you believed in all these gods?" she

asked. "The advertising gods. The parking gods. The hair gods. You have a deity for everything."

"They live inside me," he said. "They are the source of my personal power. The power to create good ads. The ability to find the killer parking spot. The confidence to wear my hair however the hell I want. The stamina to rebel. They're all here." He tapped his head. "And here." His chest.

She opened another beer and gave it to him, a wary look on her face. "So what about the relationship gods?"

He took a swig of the beer, swallowing slowly. "They're all devils," he finally said. "But the sex gods have been kind."

A flicker of something crossed her features. Disappointment? Surprise? Disdain? "They have this week," she said.

He took another drink, studying her over the bottle. "This hasn't just been all sex, Lil. I got to meet the makeover gods. Didn't even know they existed."

"The makeover *god*," she said, holding her bottle up for a mock toast, "is a goddess."

He dinged the bottle. "Is she ever."

She smiled at the compliment. "All right, then. What's the ceremony?"

"First I strip."

She looked to the heavens. "I should have known."

"All good pagan rituals are performed naked," he countered.

She took a deep drink of the lager, then screwed the glass bottle into some soft sand to hold it upright. From her jacket pocket she pulled out the washcloth-swaddled scissors.

"All right. Let's get this ceremony started." She cleared

her throat and pointed straight ahead. "Stand in front of me, pagan. I need to strip you naked."

"These gods *really* like me."

She put the scissors on the sand, then unzipped his jacket and pushed it off his shoulders. "Everyone really likes you, Jack. That's your gift."

"Do you?" He knew she did. But he wanted to hear. Wanted to see how far she'd go in admitting her feelings.

"Well, I don't know." She tugged at the bottom of his T-shirt and he helped her pull it over his head, the autumn chill doing nothing to cool the blood that was already making a U-turn from his head and causing a distinct rise in his jeans. She placed both hands on his bare chest, splayed her fingers and caressed his hair and hardened nipples. "I don't know if I'd call it 'like.' Maybe tolerate."

His jaw unhinged. "You *tolerate* me?"

Slowly she unsnapped and unzipped his pants. "I also lust for you. That's it. Lust."

"This is more than lust," he said huskily, the tug of arousal already starting to squeeze his lower half.

"You're right. This is lust plus." She glanced down at his feet. "You didn't wear shoes."

He wiggled his toes. "I don't need no—"

"Stinkin' shoes." They finished it together, laughing as she pushed the jeans over his hips and he sprang free.

"And no stinkin' underwear, I see." Her gaze moved to his erection, reminding him of the first time they'd made love, of how she'd tasted him, how instant the connection had been between them. In the past week it had only increased exponentially.

She pushed the jeans all the way down and for a minute he thought—hoped—she would drop to her knees and take him in her mouth. But she just helped him kick them off with her own feet, then bent to pick up the scissors.

Putting both hands on his shoulders, she said, "Kneel down."

He did, placing his face directly in front of her zipped hooded sweatshirt. He could slide that puppy down using nothing but his teeth. However, he remained still.

She lifted one strand of hair, the tendril that fell over his eyes and grazed his jaw. The one he knew she liked the best.

"Close your eyes," she ordered.

He did, and heard the sound of metal scraping metal as the scissors opened.

"Here you go, ye gods of hair. Gods of beauty. Gods of ridiculously sexy, hot, attractive, ought-to-be-illegal long-haired men put on earth to make women weak and helpless and panting for more."

He bit back a laugh. "You should be in advertising."

"Shhh. This is serious."

"So is advertising." He squinted through one eye, directly at her zipper.

"This hair we thusly sacrifice so that the uptight, ultra-conservative, colorless owners of Anderson, Sturgeon and Ignoble will sign the contract to make Reggie Wilding happy and subsidize a cure for Sam and transform one of the hair gods' greatest creations, Jackson Locke, into a picture-perfect ad agency president."

The shears snapped and a single golden strand floated in front of him and landed on the curve of her breast. He opened his eyes and reached for it, but instead of brushing it off, he unzipped her sweatshirt. She let him, and in a moment it fell to the ground, taking the hair with it.

She snipped another, with no funny prayer this time, more intent on doing her job right. While she did, he unbuttoned her blouse. She started on the other side, pausing long enough to let him take her shirt off.

She clipped around his ears.

He removed her bra.

She trimmed some from the side.

He opened her jeans and slid them down.

She layered along the other side.

He took her panties off.

And just as she finished trimming the front and sides, the moon slid out from a cloud and spotlighted her, with the same sucker-punch impact he'd felt the first time she'd stepped out of that shower bathed in lightning.

"Lily," he whispered, tracing one finger along the delicious rise of her hardened nipple. "You really are gorgeous."

"Turn around," she said softly.

"No way." He closed his fingers over one breast, leaning forward, openmouthed, to taste the other.

She dipped out of reach. "I have to do the back."

With a sigh of resignation, he turned on his knees and let her finish with fast, sure clips as featherlight hairs drifted over his bare skin, until the blanket he knelt on was a field of gold.

"All right, you can turn around."

He did, and she gasped a little. "Oh."

"Oh horrible or oh okay?"

Wordlessly she knelt in front of him, tossing the scissors aside. "Oh…perfect."

He wanted to remind her he was so not perfect, but she cupped his jaw with two hands, tunneling into what was left of his hair.

"You're still the best-looking man on the planet, Jack."

Her eyes were nearly black with arousal, her cheeks flushed, her lips slightly parted with breaths that were already as tight as his.

"C'mere." Pulling her body into his, feeling her heart hammer the same tattoo as his, he kissed her forehead, her eyes, and whispered in her ear. "Love me, Lil."

She closed her eyes and just before he kissed her, she whispered, "I do, Jack. I do."

The words kicked him in the gut and he almost grunted, but her kiss drowned out the sound as they tumbled onto the blanket and rolled over the remnants of his hair, instantly on their way to a familiar ecstasy.

Like a magician, she produced one of his condoms. Had that been in her jacket pocket? The echo of her two words hung on the salty air as she slid it between her teeth.

I do.

What exactly did she mean by that?

"Lily." He murmured her name, rolling her one more time so that he was on top of her. She looked up at him, strands of his cut hair caught and tangled in the thick black locks of hers.

She tore the condom wrapper open like a tigress and placed it on the edge of her tongue. Heat shot up his erection in anticipation of her mouth.

"Wait," he said.

She looked surprised, but he leaned closer and plucked a single blond hair from her eyelash. "That's about to blind you."

"Sit up," she said. He knelt and she crunched forward, used her mouth to put the condom on him and her lips to slide it down. He couldn't help smiling.

And wondering if this was *the last time* she'd referred to that morning. The last time.

Wasn't that the inevitable?

Wasn't that the curse of the *relationship* gods…if there were such a thing?

She lay back, inched her knees higher and offered him her body. "Please, Jack. Love me."

The response was on his lips, in his head, screaming out from his heart.

I do. Oh, God, I do.

"Lily," he said instead, his voice raw with need and desire and way too much emotion.

She glided her hands up his arms, over his shoulders, to his head, feathering his new short hair with gentle strokes.

"It's okay," she whispered, as though she could read his mind and sense his torture. "This is enough."

Was it?

Locked on her gaze, he slowly entered her, then lowered his head to kiss her and match the movement with tender strokes of his tongue.

He watched his reflection in her dark eyes, the image of a new man with strange hair and an even more unfamiliar pressure in his heart.

But the other, far more familiar pressure built gradually, without frenzy, without the fury that usually accompanied their orgasms. Tonight they rocked slowly, their breathing labored but rhythmic, their kisses slow and passionate, their pleasure completely mutual.

He felt her tighten around him, clasp his arms and arch her back.

"Now, Jack, now," she whispered, tightening her envelope around him. "Love me now."

The plea put him right over the edge. His climax started from so deep that it racked his whole being, shook him, shattered him until all he could do was cling to Lily and let out a long, helpless moan of pleasure and satisfaction and love.

Mostly love.

He dropped his head onto her chest, her pulse hammering against his ear, her frayed breaths torn from her lungs.

Love?

Man, he had to give her credit. The Agent of Change had certainly done her job.

Lily gave the umbrella a quick shake as she and Jack hustled into the lobby, out of the downpour that soaked Manhattan. She eyed his suit critically. She could see that it pulled a little across his back. Still, the designer threads fit well enough, and he looked every bit the agency president she'd groomed him to play.

He guided her through an unassuming lobby to a bank of older elevators, his hand on her shoulder.

"I feel like we dressed up like Deuce and Kendra for Halloween," he said, stabbing the call button. "Reggie owes us so big."

Lily smoothed Kendra's dark skirt and glanced at the open-toed heels she'd barely squeezed into. "Reggie owes *you*," she corrected. "He's already paid me."

"You get extra for agreeing to come to New York with me," he said as the elevator doors opened to a small, empty car.

It hadn't taken much convincing. It had been simple enough to borrow some of Kendra's clothes and get on the plane in Boston, telling herself she was there because she wanted to see her job through to the end.

The truth, however, was that she wanted to postpone saying goodbye to Jack as long as humanly possible. The real truth was that she harbored the secret hope that they wouldn't have to say goodbye at all. That somehow there was a way for him to be free and her to be secure. Together.

In the cold, fluorescent light of a rickety elevator, that dream seemed impossible. But last night, in the moonlight, under the stars, out in the wide open night, in Jack's strong arms with his heart matching hers beat for beat, absolutely anything had seemed possible.

He raked his newly shorn hair one more time and clenched his jaw.

"You're going to do fine," she said with a low dose of comfort in her voice.

He threw her a surprised look. "I'm not worried about this meeting."

She touched his shoulder, feeling the tensed muscles under the wool of the high-end suit. "Then what are you worried about?"

He closed his eyes for a moment, then gave her a hard look. "If this works, you get something you want. A lot. And so does Reggie. That's good. People I…people I care about are happy."

She searched his face, waiting for the "but" that she knew was coming. He said nothing, stabbing the ninth-floor button again.

"But if it works," she finished for him, "you have a job you don't want."

The car dipped to a stop, taking her stomach on a little ride while she waited for his response.

"Yeah," he said quietly, then he lightly grazed her chin with his knuckles, his expression softening. "But that's not your problem, Lil. You've done your job. Come on," he said as the doors opened to a narrow hallway. "I'll show you Wild Marketing."

At the end of the hall, double glass doors bore the engraved insignia of a *W* and the word *wild* in all lowercase. Inside a spare and hip-looking lobby, a young woman wearing a wireless headset sat at a sleek oak-and-smoked-glass counter, tapping a computer. She turned when Jack opened the door, her face blank for a second before her mouth opened so wide her chin practically hit her keyboard.

"Oh, my God! I didn't recognize you, Jack!" She stood, shock registering on her face as she pushed the headset closer to her mouth. "Wait until you see Jack Locke. You will absolutely die. He looks like another man."

Lily's heart tumbled around and landed in the vicinity of Kendra Monroe's borrowed shoes.

But Jack just cocked his head in acknowledgment. "Don't make me show you my tattoo to prove it's me, Ev."

She looked a little relieved at the crack, as though it really proved he wasn't an impostor.

"Lily, this is Evelyn Simons, office manager extraordinaire." He breezed across the lobby, peeked over her desk and grabbed a stack of messages, then indicated Lily with a wave of his hand. "Ev, meet Lily Harper, consultant without equal."

The women exchanged greetings, then Jack whisked Lily through a set of double doors, where the sparse decor continued into a small sea of cubicles and a glass wall of enclosed offices.

"This is where account managers work," he explained.

One by one, people stood to see over the cubicle walls, phones were dropped and gasps were heard and a palpable rumble of shock waves rolled through the agency.

Jack seemed totally unfazed, greeting a few people with knuckles, nodding in recognition of his changed look, but he slowed as they reached another set of double doors, and he looked expectantly at Lily.

"Reggie's office?" she asked.

"The creative department. Brace yourself."

He pushed open the doors, and instantly everything transformed. Gone was the clean, crisp atmosphere of professionalism. Gone were the cubicles and neatly lined desks and button-down collars.

Everything was bright, loud, chaotic and, well, wild. Music blared from a boom box, every surface was covered with art and color. A twentysomething girl with blue streaks in her dark hair looked up from a drafting table and blinked at Jack.

"Holy sh—"

"Shhh," he finished for her, a finger to his lips.

After more greetings, high fives, bad jokes and introductions to a staff of nine that had about sixty earrings between them—in various locations—Jack led her down one more hallway.

"Party's over now," he said as the walls changed from

pale to paneled and the hardwood floor was hushed by thick beige carpeting. "This is Mahogany Row."

Here there were not only walls, there were doors. Closed doors. Brass nameplates with titles such as Chief Financial Officer. Vice President of Human Resources. And at the far end in a large corner office, President.

Lily almost stumbled as she took in the severe surroundings, the plush, quiet seriousness so shocking after the chaos that was the creative department.

Jack could never work here. He belonged in that zoo full of music and color.

But he was going to work here. And Reggie would be happy. And Lily would have more work. And Samantha Wilding would have her husband and a chance at a rare treatment for her disease.

But Jack would be in jail for at least a year. And she was partially responsible for that imprisonment. Lily swallowed at the thought, and refused to look up at him for fear she'd beg him not to go through with it.

A severe-looking administrative assistant sat guard outside Reggie's office, but before Jack introduced them, the heavy office door swung open.

"Jack!" Reggie burst from the doorway, taking in the changes in Jack with obvious approval. "I've already heard the buzz from account management and creative. It's true. You're a new man."

"No, he's not." At Lily's emphatic interjection, they all looked at her questioningly.

"I mean, he's changed on the outside and…" she said quickly, knowing her fate for a juicy consulting contract hinged on how she handled this aspect of the job, as well.

"He's polished, yes." She reached out to greet Reggie with a handshake. "But not completely changed."

"She's being modest," Jack said, slipping past Reggie into the office. "Bring on the Brits, Reg. I'll knock their socks off. In fact…" He tugged at the knee of his trousers to reveal a dark wool ankle. "I'm actually wearing some for the occasion."

Reggie's bushy brows shot skyward as he shook Lily's hand. "Well done, Miss Harper. Well done."

Just as they settled at the round meeting table in Reggie's office, the door opened and the administrative assistant popped her head in, a worried look adding wrinkles to her brow. "Mr. Wilding. They're here."

"Thank you, Jennifer." He turned to Jack, surprise in his eyes. "They're an hour early."

Jack just shrugged. "A ploy to catch us off guard. You stay here, Lil, and get ready to pop the champagne when they leave. I'll go meet them in the lobby and bring them into the executive conference room. Reggie, you should be there, waiting for them." He glanced at Reggie, who just looked a little unhinged as he frowned at Jack. "It's professional protocol, Reg."

Lily thought her heart would explode. He was doing this for her. For Reggie. For Sam. It was a total act of selflessness, against anything he wanted to do in his heart, yet he was willing to make that sacrifice for people he cared about.

He put his hands on the table to push himself up, then froze and looked at Lily, next to him. "Here I go, Lil."

She wasn't sure she could look at him. He'd see the love on her face. God, she might even say the words. Slowly she turned to him.

"C'mere." He reached a casual hand around her neck and pulled her closer. "A kiss for luck."

He leaned toward her, but she drew back, willing the dampness in her eyes to go away. "You don't need no stinkin' luck, Jackson Locke. Every god that ever existed, or not, is on your side."

He stayed very still for a second, then closed the space between them, taking a chaste five-second kiss. "Not every one," he said quietly.

Then he stood and left the office, Reggie right behind him. For a long time she stared straight ahead, at the desk where an ad agency president worked, and tried to imagine Jack behind it.

She couldn't. She put her head in her hands, and whispered the words that had been echoing in her brain all morning.

"What have I done?"

Ten

"**Y**ou've done a tremendous job, that's what."

Lily spun around at the voice, seeing an older woman with sleek silver hair and wearing an elegant gray suit standing in the doorway.

"Think of it this way," she added. "That mammoth piece of mahogany will hide his bare feet."

Blinking, Lily stood slowly, searching her memory banks for something she knew was there but couldn't quite find. "Have we met?"

The woman glided into the room, a delicate floral scent preceding her.

"Once. But I don't think we were actually introduced. You helped my niece prepare for a job interview with a law firm in Boston, and I accompanied her to your office briefly." She held out her hand. "Samantha Wilding."

"Sam?" Lily inched back, surprised, then returned the warm handshake. "Jack speaks so highly of you."

Samantha's smile was bright, her pale blue eyes twinkling amidst a feather of crow's-feet. "My niece is Deborah Morris. Do you remember now?"

"Of course!" How could she forget the stringy-haired, awkward law student who'd been transformed into partner material? "And, yes, I do remember you." The brief meeting in Boston was coming back to her now. "It was last spring, right? Before Deborah's graduation. Isn't that right?"

"Exactly. Last March," Samantha confirmed.

"What an amazing coincidence that we've met before."

"What's amazing is the transformation you've accomplished. I just saw Jack and almost didn't recognize him."

"He certainly looks different."

"I don't mean the haircut and the expensive suit." Samantha lifted one lovely arched eyebrow as she pulled out a chair and sat, indicating for Lily to do the same. "He's in love."

Lily turned her surprised gasp into a deprecating laugh. "I don't know about that."

"I do." She crossed her arms with an air of satisfaction. "And Dorothea agrees."

Lily frowned, trying to keep up with a conversation that grew more confusing and intriguing by the second. "You mean Mrs. Slattery?"

"I'd be lost without her, of course," Samantha said, making a point of straightening a large diamond on her hand and avoiding Lily's stare. The tiniest quiver in her hands was the only giveaway that the woman battled a life-threatening illness. "She's been my eyes and ears this week."

Her eyes and ears? A slow burn started in Lily's chest, sending, she was sure, a blush to her face. What, exactly, had those eyes seen and those ears heard? She and Jack had made no effort to hide their affection...or the fact that they'd spent every night in the same bed.

Face the facts and never try to doctor up the truth—isn't that what Lily taught her clients?

"Then you know that our relationship is personal as well as professional, Mrs. Wilding."

"It's Sam." She reached across the table and closed smooth, warm fingers over Lily's hand. "And I'm thrilled this arrangement was such a success."

Lily opened her mouth to respond, then closed it, scrutinizing the lovely woman who had a little dash of devil in her sparkling eyes.

And then everything became crystal clear.

"You're the client who recommended me to Reggie, aren't you?"

"Guilty."

"And you had more than a professional makeover in mind, didn't you?"

Sam's smile was sly. "Guilty again."

"Jack thought Reggie set us up, but it was you." Lily could hardly speak as the truth washed over her. "And it was a setup."

"I can't take all the credit." Sam squeezed her hand. "Dorothea helped. But I knew you'd be perfect for him the moment I met you. I could feel it in my bones, in my heart. And I was right, wasn't I?"

Lily's arms went numb, her fingers tingled and a wave of dizziness hit so hard that she had to grip the edge of the table. This was a setup. A scheme to trap a man who would otherwise never be trapped.

Lily shifted in her seat, the right words still eluding her as it all sank in.

"Please, Lily. This really was a legitimate job and an important assignment," Sam reassured her, obviously sensing that the news wasn't being well received. "When Reggie told me about having to do something with Jack to impress the new owners, I immediately thought of you. You worked wonders with my niece. And Jack would never, ever have agreed to a standard blind date."

A tendril of anger curled around her throat, tightening it. "No, he wouldn't have."

"But I was right, wasn't I?" Sam insisted. "You two are absolutely perfect for each other."

Perfect? They were like opposing trains, headed straight for a crash on the same track.

"No," Lily said quietly. "In fact, I don't think you could have picked two people with more conflicting goals in life if you'd tried."

Sam frowned. "Sometimes opposites attract."

"Sometimes they do," she agreed. And then they clash and claw while one seeks permanence and the other seeks freedom. "In this case…" How could she describe how differently they saw the future? "We want different things out of life."

"But with Jack's new job…" Sam swept a hand toward the executive desk. "He'll be chained here. You can move to New York. Work for the ad agency. You'll be inseparable."

Lily felt her eyes open wide in horror. "I don't want to see Jack chained anywhere. I don't want to snare him. I don't want to put walls around a man who craves freedom and open spaces and a life without rules."

She stood, shaking a little, the sensation of being manipulated and used sending shock waves through her body.

"Don't you love him?" Samantha asked.

Lily almost choked. "Yes, I do."

"Well," Sam said, "so do I. And I want him to be happy."

"Happy? You don't make a man happy by forcing him into a situation he doesn't want."

"Well, I…"

Frustration and fury boiled hot as she looked at Samantha Wilding. Maybe the woman was terribly ill, maybe her intentions were noble and maybe she loved Jack in her own way, but none of that gave her the right to *manipulate* his life—and Lily's.

"He did this for you," Lily said, her voice so tight with emotion that she hissed. "He endured this whole project for you. And this is how you thank him? Trying to lasso him into a life he doesn't want? Into a place that—that could kill his spirit and his creativity and the very essence that makes Jackson Locke so remarkable and special? That very thing that makes me love him so much?"

Blood pumped violently in her ears, deafening her to any sounds around her. So she almost didn't hear the gentle clearing of a throat behind her. Then he repeated the sound, and Samantha's stunned gaze shifted to the doorway.

Lily didn't have to look. She knew who stood behind her. And she knew he'd heard every word.

Lily loved him.

The knowledge hit like a sledgehammer to Jack's chest,

making his heart pummel his ribs so hard that clearing his throat was really all he was capable of at that moment.

"Reggie left the contract on his desk," he finally said, still unable to look away from Lily.

"Jack." She looked as miserable and shocked as he felt, her complexion pale from the blood that must have rushed from her head to her heart. "You were right from the first night. It was a setup."

"So I have Sam to thank instead of Reggie." His voice was surprisingly low-key and calm, considering the tornado that whipped through his blood. "Excellent choice in companions, Sammy. Excuse me, ladies. I'm just going to grab some papers."

"Jack, listen to me." Lily could barely hide the touch of desperation in her tone. "You don't have to do this."

"I know that," he said, but he walked toward the desk and the ominous stack of papers that contained his future.

Samantha stood and reached for him as he passed the table. "You're not mad at me, Jack, are you? Lily is upset."

He evaded her outstretched hand and continued across the office. "No harm done, Sam," he assured her, without even glancing her way. "We had fun, didn't we, Lil?"

The phrase felt phony and forced, but his attention was zeroed in on the pile of legal-sized documents. He spun it around so that he could read the top page. The small print was all jargon and corporate speak, but the main message blared across the top in bold letters.

The acquisition of Wild Marketing by Anderson, Sturgeon and Noble…

Behind him, he was vaguely aware of a chair scraping, and the sound of a soft intake of breath.

"Fun?" The single syllable from Lily's lips carried a hard punch.

He blinked at the onerous words on the legal document, lifting it as he looked at her. "Didn't you have fun?"

She looked stricken. "Of course. Fun. That's what it's all about, right, Jack? No-strings fun, then on to the next good time." She nodded to Sam, whose jaw looked a little unhinged at the exchange. "A pleasure to meet you, Mrs. Wilding. Would you be kind enough to arrange for Mrs. Slattery to return all of my belongings to my office in Boston? Mr. Wilding has the address."

Jack's fingers closed around the pages as he watched Lily march to the door. Didn't she know he was up to his eyeballs in this deal he hated and couldn't take Sam to task for what was probably the greatest gift he'd ever been given?

"Lily?"

She turned to him, with the same expression she'd worn when the boom had almost hit her in the face. "Goodbye, Jack. It's been...fun." The word fell with a thud.

"No, wait!" He started to follow just as Sam leaped into his path to do the same, and Jack had to wrench back from running into her, sending a hundred pages of legal documents scattering around the room like a blizzard.

"Oh, Jack, I'm sorry!" Sam exclaimed, her arms extended as if she could possibly catch some of the flying paper.

He bit back a curse, watching helplessly as the pages of his future fluttered about and the woman of his dreams disappeared from sight.

Samantha stood just as frozen, her hands over her mouth and horror in her eyes. "I shouldn't have done that."

"No, Sam, you shouldn't have."

"What's going on, Jack? We're waiting…" Reggie's voice boomed from the hall just before he appeared in the doorway. "Oh, Lord. Is that the contract?"

"Honey, I really made a mess of things," Sam sighed.

She sure as hell had, Jack thought bitterly.

Reggie lunged toward the floor. "Jennifer! Please help us put this contract back together." He started scooping up papers, but Jack just stood still, and so did Sam.

"Jack," she said, reaching out to him. "Go get her."

He wanted to. His whole being screamed to tear into that hallway and get her before she reached the elevator.

"Please," Reggie insisted, looking up from the floor and his sea of legalese. "I need you to do this. You've come this far. They want to make the deal, Jack." Reggie's pained expression deepened as he looked at his wife. "Sam and I need this time together."

"No," Sam said, squeezing her narrow fingers over Jack's wrist. "Reggie, you're taking Jack's freedom to buy yours. That's wrong."

The crack in her voice had the same effect on Jack's heart.

"And," Sam added, her pale blue eyes moist with unshed tears, "I was wrong to try and play matchmaker."

"Actually," Jack said, fighting the urge to reach out and dry Sam's tears, "you nailed it, Sammy. She's the one for me." Just saying it out loud felt so good. "I'm in love with her."

Reggie stood slowly and Sam drew back. "You are?" they asked in perfect, married-for-thirty-years unison.

"I am."

They beamed at each other, also in unison, making Jack smile despite the ache that filled him. "You two are quite a team."

"That's called marriage," Sam said softly. "You might give it a try sometime."

"Well, what are you doing here?" Reggie gave Jack's other arm a soft shove.

Sam nodded, adding pressure to the other arm. "Go, Jack."

Jack took one second to reach down and kiss Sam's cheek. "I owe you one, Sammy." He turned to Reggie. "Stall the suits. I'll be back."

"No," Reggie said, shaking his head. "I'll tell them the truth."

"That I'm leaving?"

"That the only thing that matters at an ad agency is the quality of the creative. And we've got that covered. With the best damn creative director in the business." Reggie gave him one more push. "Go!"

Jack needed no more encouragement to hustle into the hall and zip through the departments of Wild Marketing, ignoring the strange looks from his colleagues.

He had to get Lily.

The elevator was gone, the hall was empty. He considered the stairs, but pounded on the call button and hissed "Yesss!" when it dinged down.

She'd misunderstood him, that's all. He punched the lobby level button six times, the thought bellowing in his head. She'd totally misunderstood him.

He'd been so preoccupied with the meeting and the contract and the role he was playing that he hadn't even thought about what he said.

It was fun.

What an *idiot*.

He practically shoved the elevator doors wide open as

he burst into the lobby and scanned the empty area. Outside the glass doors, torrential rain turned the streets of Manhattan into a waterfall, driving almost all the pedestrians inside.

Had she gotten into a cab already?

Throwing open the main door, he jogged onto the sidewalk, squinting left and right into the downpour and seeing almost no one on the street. A dark movement about a block away caught his attention. Was that her?

With a silent apology to Deuce for ruining a perfectly good two-thousand-dollar suit, he tore out into the rain, jumping a few puddles, holding off an oncoming cab at the corner and keeping his focus on the dark figure that walked slowly through the rain.

He saw her fling back a lock of sodden hair, and joy punched his chest. It was her. It was *her*.

"Lily!" he called.

She almost faltered, then continued, upping her speed. Was she really going to run away from him like this?

"Lily!" He broke into a jog and reached her in less than fifty steps, slowing only as he could make out the individual strands of hair and the familiar, feminine way she walked.

Finally she stopped, turning slowly, the sight of her like a punch in the gut.

"This is just how I found you," he said, dropping to a slow walk to approach her. "Soaking wet and absolutely beautiful."

She pushed limp, wet hair from her eyes, lifting her chin despite the way it quivered. "So this is how you can remember me."

"Lily, are you crazy?" He couldn't stop himself. He

reached for her, sinking his fingers into the waterlogged shoulders of her jacket. "How can you walk away from this?"

She blinked at the rain, the remnants of makeup making her expression look even more tortured. God, he hoped it was the rain. He couldn't stand to know he'd made her cry.

"I'm so sorry, Lil. I really didn't mean what I said up there."

"Don't, Jack. You have enough handcuffs around your wrists now. And I did my part to help put them there. I'm the one who owes you an apology. I just sort of lost it. I was so stunned at what Sam did, and then—"

"Listen to me." He squeezed tighter, pulled her closer. "I just told Reggie no. The deal's off. Or maybe it's on. I don't know. But it won't include me as agency president. I'm free of that."

She tried to ease out of his grip, but he wouldn't let go. "Good, that's great. That's the right thing. I need to get a cab to the airport." She glanced out on the New York street where, for once, there were no cars or cabs. The gods were on his side here. For the moment, anyway.

"I'll go with you," he said quickly. "I'm done here. Let's fly to Boston, get back to Nantucket and figure this out."

She managed to escape his grasp. "Figure what out?"

"Lily." Undeterred, he dug his hands under her hair, tunneling into the last dry place on her. "I love you. And I heard what you said. You love me right back."

She opened her mouth in shock, then closed it, just managing to slip out of his grip. "No, Jack."

"You don't?"

"I do," she said. "I do. And that's what hurts so much.

Loving you can only mean heartache. You can't stay with one woman indefinitely."

"We'll make it work," he insisted. "We can do anything together. Look what we've done this week. You take days, I'll take nights. We'll have—"

She put her hand over his mouth. "We'll have sex and fun and laughs and joyrides through the cranberry bogs and sacrifices to your gods. We'll have a blast. But we won't have what I want, even if you did manage to settle down with one woman. If I don't experience that heartbreak, then there's the little issue of your no-boundaries, no-walls, no-limits lifestyle. I can't live like that. I can't. You know that."

A car rumbled by and shot a spray of rainwater at them, punctuating her statement and leaving him speechless.

"What we'll have," she continued, "is a good time. That's what you are all about, Jack. From the beginning I've known it, and still, still…" She fought a break in her voice, and the water in her eyes wasn't rain. "I fell for you. Knowing all along that eventually you'll have to escape the restrictions of a relationship. Fully aware that you crave autonomy and freedom and a life without walls. I fell in love with you anyway."

He wanted to throw his arms into the air and howl with happiness. "Lily, honey, that's all we need. We can make this work."

"No, Jack. You know what I want, and you know why I want it. I want walls that never come down. I want so many boundaries that I am wrapped in a lifelong security blanket. I want a home that lasts for generations, a yard full of children and rooms full of *stuff* that I never have to part with."

What compromises could he make? He'd do anything,

anything to stay with Lily. "I could live any way you want as long as I'm with you."

"No, you *can't*." It was more of a sob than a word. "You say that now, Jack. You believe that because you think you're in love. But I know you. You'll thrash about like a fish on a hook and I will know that I was the one who reeled you in. I stole you from your life of freedom. I could never be happy knowing that you're unhappy. I knew that up there in the office." She took a deep breath and reached up, wiping rain from his freshly shaved cheeks. "I love you too much to force you into something you don't want."

He drew her in to him, trying to swallow the boulder in his throat. He couldn't. He just choked and leaned down to kiss her. To stop the words that hurt…because they were true.

"Fundamentally, you know I'm right, don't you?" she asked.

Was she? Was he just fooling himself to think that one woman—one rain-washed, heart-wrenching, beautiful woman—could really change Jack Locke?

There had to be something he could say to her. To himself.

Searching her face, he considered, and then discarded, every possible response. There was no tagline that would fix this. No joke, no funny comeback, no single line of defense. Because she was right. He'd never change.

And that was going to cost him the best woman in the world.

She lifted herself on her tiptoes and kissed his cheek. "Bye." A cab rolled up next to them, and a woman climbed out of the back, flicking an umbrella open.

Lily waved at the driver. Jack grasped her outstretched fingertips as though he could hold on to her, but she slipped away, darted into the backseat and looked up at him just as she was about to close the door.

She put her fingers on her lips and blew him a quick kiss. "I'll never forget you."

The cab sped away with a vicious spurt that drenched his suit. But Jack didn't move. He stood in the rain, watching the spot of yellow blend into the New York City traffic until it disappeared around the next corner.

Jackson Locke was a completely free man. No boundaries, no rules, no job he didn't want, no woman to tie him down, no piece of paper that tied him to anyone legally or otherwise.

The gods, as always, had given him exactly what he wanted.

And it hurt like hell.

Eleven

When Lily unlocked her office door the phone was already ringing, sending a glimmer of hope through her. God, she could use some new business. The winter had been brisk, but things slowed down in March and she'd barely made her rent on the five-hundred-square-foot store-front in Waltham.

Dreams of moving into space in downtown Boston, or even a closer-in suburb, were getting more distant. And she'd just made herself more frustrated by going to see that little house in Framingham on Saturday. Sure, she could make the down payment, but the mortgage? The thought of the bank wolf howling at her door made her stomach churn.

She reached for the phone and automatically slipped into her faux assistant voice. "Good morning, The Change Agency. This is Nan. Can I help you?"

Nan. For Nantucket, of course. Some dreams, it seemed, died harder than others.

"May I speak to Lily Harper, please?"

She wasn't at all surprised the caller asked for her—she was the only employee. But the heavy British accent threw her.

"Of course, sir. May I tell Miss Harper who is calling?"

"Bryce Noble. From London."

Lily dropped into her seat, gripping the receiver. Bryce Noble? Of Anderson, Sturgeon and *Ig*noble?

"May I tell her what this is regarding?"

"This is about new business. Is she taking any at the moment?"

She sure wasn't turning any away. "Just a moment, Mr. Noble. I'll get Ms. Harper for you."

She pressed the hold button and let the receiver fall onto the desk. New business? She'd never returned Reggie's calls after she'd left New York six months earlier. Once he'd had Samantha try; that was when Lily hired "Nan" to screen calls. Not that she would have screened them *all*. But to no one's real surprise, Jack had never even called once.

With a quick clearing of her throat, Lily became Lily again.

"This is Lily Harper."

"Ms. Harper, my name is Bryce Noble and I'm the worldwide creative director of Anderson, Sturgeon and Noble." Yep, it was Ignoble himself.

"How can I help you, Mr. Noble?"

"I understand you are an extraordinary performance coach with some notable successes to your credit. Several of your clients have highly recommended your work."

Several meaning Sam and Reggie Wilding, no doubt, who still probably wallowed in guilt for causing her heartbreak and promising her business that she'd been too proud to accept.

"Why are you calling me?" The question sounded abrupt, but protocol be damned. Even this distant connection with Jack Locke was causing heart palpitations she didn't want.

"I'm calling to offer you a substantial assignment."

She inhaled deeply, trying to dig for the resolve that had gotten her through the first few wretched months after she said goodbye to Jack on a rainy afternoon in New York.

She'd sworn she would never do any work for that agency—maybe any ad agency—because the risk of seeing him was too great. It would take one moment, one kiss, one finger comb through hair that had undoubtedly grown back by now for her to melt and give in. Then she was facing either eventual heartbreak or the footloose life that went against everything she'd ever dreamed of.

Jack wouldn't change…and neither would she.

"This is a very busy time for my business," she said, her gaze falling on a totally empty calendar page. She picked up a pen to write something on it. Anything.

She scrawled "clean coffeemaker" on today's date.

"I'm sorry," she continued. "The Change Agency is completely booked right now. I doubt I'll be able to help you on a large assignment."

"It would entail performance coaching of executives," he continued, undaunted by her rejection. "In every one of our twenty-seven offices."

"Twenty-six," she corrected without thinking, her pen

taking on a life of its own as she wrote a four-figure number and multiplied it by twenty-six.

"Actually, we have twenty-seven since our acquisition in New York City."

She scratched the math. "Yes, Wild Marketing." Her heart inched up her chest to park itself in her throat. She could never consider this job. Not if Jack was still in any way, shape or form connected to the company. But if he wasn't…

"So how is that merger coming along, Mr. Noble?"

"Excellent, thank you. We've assimilated the Wild group nicely into ours and have brought on a number of new clients."

"And in New York, the president…" Her voice trailed off and she squeezed her eyes shut. Why was she doing this to herself? If she wanted to know what had happened, all she had to do was search the company name on the Internet. And she'd avoided that temptation. Daily.

"We brought in a new management team and one of our British executives is running that office now."

Had Jack really quit? "And has the creative team changed?"

"One of the art directors was promoted to creative director to fill the void when Jackson Locke left the company."

She actually exhaled with relief. He was gone. He'd moved on, maybe opened his own shop, or found another agency that let him be himself. Wherever he was, he was free, unencumbered and, she deeply hoped, happy.

She wrote that four-figure number again. Multiplied by twenty-seven. Pictured the house in Framingham.

"So what exactly did you have in mind for the performance coaching, Mr. Noble? Perhaps I can clear a little bit of time for you."

"You'd have to clear a year."

"A year? That does sound like a major undertaking."

"It's a massive project, Ms. Harper, and I'd like to have you fly to London to meet with my team and discuss our needs. All expenses paid, of course. Once we agree on a fee and schedule, then you would be spending two weeks at every office for the next year. I'm afraid it would mean living out of hotels for a year, but I assure you we will make it worth your while."

A year on the road. No home. No office. No other business. But in the end, enough for a down payment so sizable, her mortgage payments would be far less than her rent.

"When would you like to meet, Mr. Noble?"

"Does that mean you can clear your calendar?"

She fluttered the pages of her desk calendar. "I'll have Nan start making the necessary calls right away."

"Excellent. Can you be here this Wednesday afternoon, at the office in London? We'll arrange for your travel and accommodations."

"I think I can do that. And thank you, Mr. Noble."

"It's Bryce," he said, a quick laugh softening the British accent. "We're pretty casual in the creative department."

"Yes." She closed her eyes. "I remember that."

She remembered everything, she thought as she hung up.

Although she'd gotten the time lost on memory lane down to less than an hour a day. Would working in advertising set her back to the old three- or four-hour bouts of self-imposed misery and Jack wallowing?

No matter. In one year she'd easily have enough to buy a house. If not the one she'd seen this weekend, then some other house. She'd put a fence around the yard, get a dog, maybe a kitten or two and a garden and window treatments, and she'd paint every blessed wall a beautiful color.

And then she'd bounce off them.

No, she chided herself, standing up to start the process of her new life. Once she had her home, her yard, her security, all her loneliness would disappear. Wouldn't it?

She pondered that question endlessly for the next two days. As she made the arrangements to go to London, packed her bags, took a cab to Logan Airport, settled comfortably in first class and flew across the Atlantic Ocean, she wondered when the loneliness would go away.

With each mile she traveled closer to the offices that at one time she'd thought Jack might frequent, she let herself think about him. When the pain got too great, she remembered that at least he wouldn't be there. She'd known that for certain when, in preparation for this meeting, she'd run a search on the agency and had seen no employee by the name of Jackson Locke.

When she checked in to an upscale, elegant hotel not far from the agency headquarters and stared out at the streets of London, she couldn't help but wonder what it would have been like if she hadn't gotten into that cab and ridden away from the one and only man she'd ever loved.

She'd either be the happiest woman on earth right now, or even more dejected. Knowing Jack Locke? Her money was on dejected. Six months would have pushed his statute of limitations on a relationship, and their love affair would have died as fast and furiously as it had started. Or she would be aching for permanence and security and walls... and he'd be having none of it.

No, there was no future—at least no chance of the one she wanted—with Jack.

When the limo pulled up in front of the main entrance of the hotel, Lily tamped down the last of her second thoughts and regrets. This was the start of an entire new life. This was the six-figure assignment she'd dreamed of when she first opened the door to Reggie's Nantucket estate and nearly melted at the sight of "the pool boy."

Smoothing her skirt, offering her best smile, she entered the grandiose offices of Anderson, Sturgeon and Noble, announced herself and waited for Bryce Noble.

When the door was flung open, she fought a smile of surprise. She'd expected fifty, gray and businesslike. But she got thirty-five, shaved head and a bright red T-shirt over jeans. He looked, ironically enough, as if he'd just stepped out of the creative department at Wild Marketing.

Maybe Jack had been too hasty.

"Lily, welcome to London." Bryce shook her hand warmly and guided her into the hall. "Let's go into this conference room. Did you have a good trip? Hotel okay?"

"Wonderful, thank you." She glanced around the empty corridor. "Is the creative department nearby? I'd love to see it."

"I'll take you on a tour later," he promised her. "It's always the most interesting part of any agency."

As he reached for the conference-room door, she glanced down, taking in his sockless feet stuffed into scuffed loafers.

Jack wouldn't have hated it here, after all.

The irony of that thought squeezed her heart, but she pushed it away.

"I hope you don't mind that I've invited another consultant," Bryce said as he pulled the door open.

She barely heard him. She *had* to stop thinking about Jack. Jack was gone. Jack was over. Jack was a crazy, wild, unforgettable joyride through a cranberry bog. Jack was—

Jack was *there*.

"Oh."

That one syllable told him everything he needed to know.

The gods still loved him, and so did Lily Harper.

"Hey, Lil."

She froze in the doorway, her beautiful mouth in the shape of her single word, her eyes just as wide, the color draining, then rushing back to her cheeks.

And he loved her, too.

"What are you doing here?" she demanded.

He threw a look at Bryce. "That's an American expression for 'it's great to see you.'"

Bryce just laughed, as Jack knew he would. If it hadn't been for Bryce Noble, one man who had an even more sarcastic sense of humor than Jack, he'd have sailed out of the newly formed agency the day Reggie signed his papers and took his check. But Bryce had figured out a way to keep him.

"I'm a consultant," Jack explained, fighting the urge to hurdle the table that separated them and pull her so deep into his chest that she could feel his heart leap with happiness at the sight of her. "Just like you."

"I'm not committed to that yet," she said quickly, putting a nervous hand on her professional updo and taking a step backward.

Jack watched the move with a wry smile. "You know, if my lessons in body language hadn't been taught by an expert, I might not notice that you're trying to bolt out the door." He stood and indicated the chair across from him. "I think you ought to stay and hear us out."

"Us?" Thankfully she took another step closer. "So you knew I'd be here today?"

Bryce eased her into the room. "Of course he did. Jack has been the driving force behind the makeover we're about to discuss with you and adamant that no one else is qualified to undertake the job. I understand you did a marvelous job with him."

She regarded him again, her gaze narrowing as she examined hair that easily covered his ears and grazed his jaw again, then zeroed in on the tuft of hair he'd grown under his chin. He tweaked it with pride. "And wait'll you see my new tattoo."

"Please, have a seat, Lily," Bryce offered, pulling out the chair directly across from Jack.

"I thought you hated this," Lily said, indicating the surroundings with one hand. "Hated everything about this kind of agency."

"I thought so, too," he said, grinning at Bryce. "And, to be honest, Anderson is a stiff and Sturgeon is a bore."

"Crashing," Bryce agreed.

"But Bryce, here, turned out to be a pretty cool guy."

"Thank you, mate."

"And, even better," Jack said, leaning forward just so he had a slim chance of getting a whiff of that sweet perfume she used to wear, "Bryce likes what I have to offer."

"What Jack has to offer," Bryce said as he sat, "includes

a highly unorthodox reformation of twenty-seven creative directors and their staffs."

Jack gave her a warm smile and got a flicker of response in return. A flicker. He could work with that. "And that's where you, Lily Harper, agent of change, come in."

"Our problem," Bryce said, "is that we have a very old-school mind-set in our creative departments around the globe. I'd like to change that. As soon as I met Jack and we started to work on some creative together—"

"I thought you quit," she interrupted suddenly, obviously still processing a situation she'd never anticipated. "I thought you left the company when it bought Wild."

"I did."

"But I convinced him to consult," Bryce added, then lifted his lips in a dry smile. "At a ridiculously high price, I might add."

"Then why didn't you…"

Call.

The unspoken word might as well have been screamed.

"I've been very busy," he said, ignoring her dubious expression. He *had* been busy. And he wouldn't call, write or show up at her door until he had everything in place and proof that he'd changed.

And now he did.

He tried to tell her that with one meaningful look, but she turned to Bryce.

"We're looking for you to help coach our creative people in a slightly different way than you usually do," Bryce told her, pretending not to be aware of the dynamics ricocheting between them. "We want them all to loosen up a bit. Drop the suits, ties and wingtips, you know?"

She looked from one to the other. "I usually work in the other direction. I tend to tighten people up, not loosen them."

"You *change* people," Jack said softly. "I'm living proof."

Before she could argue, Bryce pushed himself from the conference table.

"I'm going to let you think about it, Lily. Talk to Jack for a few minutes. I'll be back with some paperwork, fee schedules and details for you to consider."

Bryce left them alone and Jack didn't waste a second. He reached across the table and closed two hands over the ones she'd kept clasped in front of her. The first skin-to-skin contact he'd had with her in six months—with any woman, to be fair—sent a shock wave through him.

"You look great, Lily," he said. "I miss you."

She paled at the words. "Do you live here now, in London?"

"I don't live anywhere. Not yet, anyway."

"Of course you don't," she said quickly, drawing her hands away from his touch. "That's a perfect life for you."

"I wouldn't call it perfect," he said with a soft laugh at his own understatement. "There's plenty of room for improvement."

She nodded, as though she understood. "Well, I'm really glad this all worked out for you in the end." For a long moment she just stared at him, trying so hard to swallow he could see her struggle.

"Nothing's worked out for me. And nothing's ended yet."

"Of course it has. You consult and travel and hang out with other cool creative types. You have no day-to-day responsibilities, no employees, no worries, no home, no problems."

"I have plenty of problems," he corrected.

She pushed out from the table. "I'm happy for you."

She hadn't heard him. And even if she had, nothing was sinking in.

"Lily," he said, standing at the same time she did, "I need to show you something."

"No, thank you." Her voice was tight with emotion and he saw her clench and release one hand. Hadn't she taught him that was a sign of self-protection?

"I think it's time to pull out my trump card."

"Save your trump card, Jack. Nothing's changed."

"Everything's changed." He zipped around the table, blocking her way to the door and taking her hand again. "Come with me, Lily. I want to show you something."

"No, thanks."

"Maybe you'll be interested in this." He put his fingers on the snap of his jeans and she jerked back, looking shocked.

"Keep your trump card in your pants, Jack. I'm not interested."

He smiled at that, tilting his head. "I just want to show you my new tattoo."

She almost laughed, then let her gaze drop. "Sure. I'll call your bluff. Show me."

He unzipped his fly less than half an inch, then folded the corner of the jeans down over his lower stomach to reveal his new ink. "What do you think?"

She stared at the design, her jaw loose, her gaze riveted. "It's a lily."

"Yep. And it's permanent." He zipped up before his body responded to the proximity and smell and admiring gaze of the woman he loved.

"That's it?" She half choked. "You think you can keep

me here just because you went out and got a tattoo? That's your trump card?"

"No." He reached into his pocket, pulled out a key and dangled it in front of her. "This is."

Twelve

"Where are we going?"

Lily slid her hand into Jack's because the streets of London were crowded and unfamiliar, and because he'd broken into a near jog since they'd left the conference room ten minutes ago. Not because it felt so utterly blissful to hold his hand again.

"We're going to the bank."

"The bank?" Why in God's name were they going to the bank? But she didn't ask. Instead, she inhaled the scents of a foreign country, speed walking past the high-end flats and upscale clothing shops of Knightsbridge. Cars whizzed by—on the wrong side of the road—and nannies rumbled strollers in their path.

Jack bounded toward his destination like a man on a

mission, never letting Lily get more than two inches from his side.

No matter that this was all wrong and dizzyingly confusing, it felt so good and so right to be with Jack that Lily had to fight to keep from skipping and throwing her arms around him and dancing for the unadulterated joy of being on one of his wild rides again.

Instead, she checked out the sights and held tight to his large, warm hand. At the entrance to a building bearing the insignia of Moneycorp Bank, he held the heavy glass door for her. "After you, Lil."

No one else ever called her *Lil*. It still made her legs weak.

"Are we making a deposit or picking one up?"

"Neither."

"Then why are we here?"

He paused in front of a tall information counter and set the gold key down, letting it snap on the gleaming wood and yanking the guard to attention.

"Safe deposit boxes, please."

"Just a moment, sir," the guard said in a thick British accent.

While they waited, Jack took her other hand and inched her closer to him.

"Brace yourself," he whispered.

Chills cartwheeled down her spine.

The guard returned, hustled them to another part of the bank, checked Jack's ID and, in less than five minutes, they were alone in a small room lined with safe deposit boxes and almost filled by one large table in the center.

Jack went purposefully to one box, inserted the key and

opened a drawer, then pulled out a long, thick roll of documents fastened with a rubber band.

"I told you I've been busy," he said.

Lily squeezed her hands into fists. "Doing what?"

He smoothed a large piece of paper on the table, drawing her attention to the blue lines and square slanted writing.

Blueprints.

"What is this?"

"This, my love, is a home."

"A home?" *My love.* The chills shuddered through her whole body now. "Whose home?"

He looked up from the paper, his emerald eyes so serious and penetrating. "Ours."

She couldn't do anything but stare at him.

He reached for her. "C'mere. Look."

Taking his hand, she let him guide her around the table to stand next to him. Taking a steadying breath, she looked at the blueprints. Of a home.

Ours.

"This is the front elevation."

Gabled windows, a sloped roofline, a glorious widow's walk across the top was all she could take in. "It's…pretty." Pretty amazing.

"I think so." He flipped to the next page. "This is the first floor. That's the family room, which is really big, as you can see. And the kitchen, and that veranda runs the perimeter of the house. See?"

Lily could feel Jack's gaze move from the blueprints to her, gauging her reaction, waiting for her words. But all she could do was place a finger on the drawing and travel over the thin blue sketches of the house.

Ours.

She blinked to focus on the lettering. Formal living room. Office. Library. Media room.

He turned over the large paper to reveal more. "This is the second floor." She could hear the excitement in his voice. "Check out that master. Massive, huh? And all those bedrooms are designed to be in hearing distance…in case anyone…anyone small…needs something at night."

The lump in her throat cut off her air and the blueprint floated as her eyes welled. "Uh-huh," she managed.

"And this is the best part." He turned to the last page. "The third floor is pretty much all glass. This is an art studio. And office and meeting rooms in case I have clients in."

"All windows," she said, her voice husky. "No walls."

"And here's the view," he said as if he could read her mind. "Actually, this is the view from everywhere in the house."

He slowly turned the last page, to a layout of large photographs. At first all she could see was red, burgundy and bright maroon.

For a moment she thought the water in the pictures was moving, but that was only because she was looking at the cranberry bog through tears.

"This is the view from that hill," she said, finally looking up at him. "Over the bog. Where we had our first picnic at night."

"That's where we're going to build our house."

Our house.

"But you said it was owned by some…" Her voice trailed off. "Somebody with more money than time. Who… How did you…?"

His eyes answered the question. *He* was that somebody.

"I bought that parcel of land when Reggie bought his house in Nantucket, about eight years ago. Now that I'm consulting, I have the time. And…" He took her hand and closed it in both of his. "I want to build this home for you. For us."

She knew if she blinked, the tears would pour. So she looked down at the photos, and the first drop hit the page with a splat. Jack placed his finger on the tear and smeared it.

"Lily," he whispered. "Even tears can't wash down a paper wall if the love that built them is strong enough."

She almost buckled with emotion, but in an instant he had his arms around her, pulling her so tightly into his chest she could hear his heart hammer at the same insane rate as hers.

"Please, tell me yes, Lil."

"It depends on what you're asking," she said, closing her eyes and inhaling the glorious scent of Jack. Of dreams. Of forever.

"I'm asking you to spend your life with me." He guided her chin up to face him. "I love you, Lily. I love you so much. I want you to be my wife and my partner and my lover and my best friend and the mother of my children." His voice cracked on the last one and that just about did her in.

"Jack." She drew back to look at him, stunned to see the tears he fought were as real as her own. "I love you, too."

He kissed her, gently at first, then hungrily as the ache they'd fought for six months evaporated.

"We have one year to shape this company together," he said. "During that time, we're going to build that house, travel the world, plan our future, name our babies, make our dreams and fall in love all over again."

A sense of joy so complete and total washed over Lily, and she clung to the man she loved. "Are you sure, Jack? Are you positive you want to do this?"

"Lily, I've never been so sure of anything in my life." He cupped her face and kissed a tear. "I've lived for this moment ever since you walked away in New York. I've examined my heart, and I took all sorts of time for that self-discovery you suggested."

"What did you discover?" she asked, her fingers moving automatically to the one strand of hair that hung close to his eyes.

"That I'm more whole and more happy and more free with you than without you. I want walls, Lil. If you're inside them with me, I want them all. That's the real freedom in life. The freedom to totally be yourself with the one person who loves you, and who you love."

"Ah, Jack." She slid her arms around his neck and hugged him. "I can't believe you did all this."

"I've changed, Lily."

She drew back enough to look into his eyes. "No. No, you haven't. And I don't want you to. I love you exactly the way you were and are and will be. Don't change a thing."

"I love you, too," he whispered, kissing her gently, then letting the passion rock them again.

She broke the kiss, a frown on her face. "All this in a year? Build a house, handle this assignment, plan a life and make all that love? How can we do that?"

"Easy." He nibbled at her neck and worked his way back to her mouth, easing her backward over the table. "You get the days. I get the nights."

"It's nice to know…" She kissed him lightly and slid a

loving hand through his long hair. "That some things will never change."

Jack surveyed the blanket of color that unfolded beyond the veranda, the jeweled reds and golds of early autumn in New England, warmed by an unusually powerful September sun. He inhaled deeply, the sweet scent of the cranberry bog mixing with the salt of the not-so-distant sea and the aroma of the single lily that Dots had pinned on his lapel with tears in her eyes just moments ago.

The first quiet notes of a piano melody filled the air and Jack clasped his hands together in front of him and turned toward the rows of seats.

"Nervous?"

Jack glanced to his left and gave Deuce a get-real look. "Were you?"

"Are you kidding? I was scared to death your sister would change her mind. She's the most beautiful woman in the world."

Jack smiled. "One of them."

"And there's another," Deuce said, indicating the back of the aisle with a wide smile that crinkled his eyes.

Both men beamed at the tiniest attendant, two-year-old Jacquie Monroe, toddling forward in layers of gold crinoline, a very serious look on her precious face. She stepped slowly the way they'd practiced the night before, plucking each flower petal and fluttering it to the makeshift aisle with earnest determination, sparing a glance at the audience as they let out a collective "Awwww."

Deuce and Jack shared a look, acknowledging this

passage in their lifetime of friendship, then back at the little girl. She lifted her head and her eyes locked on Deuce.

"Uh-oh," Jack whispered. "Trouble."

"Daddy!" Jacquie broke into a run and headed straight for Deuce.

"Hey." He scooped her up as the guests burst into laughter. "That's not what we practiced."

Her little face fell in shame, but Deuce eased her to the ground. "It's okay, pumpkin. You were perfect."

The little trauma over, the next beautiful woman started down the aisle. Kendra looked radiant in a burnished gold gown, her gaze, like her daughter's, locked on Deuce. As she approached the flowery altar where Jack would be married, she looked at her older brother.

"Be happy," she mouthed.

"I am," he whispered back as Kendra took her spot next to Jacquie, giving her daughter an encouraging smile.

The piano hidden around the corner suddenly paused midnote, then started the first few notes of a song Jackson Locke never really thought he'd hear. At least, not played for him.

How could he be so lucky?

She appeared around the corner, a vision in satin and cream. She curled her fingers over Reggie's arm, smiling at him, exchanging a quick word that made Reggie chuckle.

Then she turned to the woman on her left. Samantha Wilding was thin and pale, but the Swiss treatment was definitely working miracles. When Lily had asked that both the Wildings give her away, Sam had cried with joy. They made an unconventional little trio walking down the aisle, but that was precisely what Jack liked about the idea.

After all, none of this would have happened without Sam.

"Thanks, Reg," Jack said, shaking the older man's hand when they reached the minister. "And, Sammy, how can I thank you? All this time I thought the gods loved me, but it was really you."

Sam reached out, her eyes moist, her mouth quivering. "You don't need those gods anymore, Jack, because now…" She took his hand and joined it to Lily's, giving them both a squeeze. "You have an angel right here on earth."

* * * * *

Turn the page for a sneak preview
of the first book in the new miniseries
DIAMONDS DOWN UNDER
from Silhouette Desire®,
VOWS & A VENGEFUL GROOM
by Bronwyn Jameson

Available January 2008

Silhouette Desire®
Always Powerful, Passionate and Provocative

Kimberley Blackstone didn't notice the waiting horde of media until it was too late. Flashbulbs exploded around her like a New Year's light show. She skidded to a halt, so abruptly her trailing suitcase all but overtook her.

This had to be a case of mistaken identity. Surely. Kimberley hadn't been on the paparazzi hit list for close to a decade, not since she'd estranged herself from her billionaire father and his headline-hungry diamond business.

But no, it was *her* name they called. *Her* face was the focus of a swarm of lenses that circled her like avid hornets. Her heart started to pound with fear-fueled adrenaline.

What did they want?

What was going on?

With a rising sense of bewilderment she scanned the crowd for a clue, and her gaze fastened on a tall, leonine figure forcing his way to the front. A tall, familiar figure. Her head came up in stunned recognition, and their gazes collided across the sea of heads before the cameras erupted with another barrage of flashes, this time right in her exposed face.

Blinded by the flashbulbs—and by the shock of that momentary eye-meet—Kimberley didn't realize his intent until he'd forged his way to her side, possibly by the sheer strength of his personality. She felt his arm wrap around her shoulder, pulling her into the protective shelter of his body, allowing her no time to object. No chance to lift her hands to ward him off.

In the space of a hastily drawn breath, she found herself plastered knee-to-nose against six feet two inches of hard-bodied male.

Ric Perrini.

Her lover for ten torrid weeks, her husband for ten tumultuous days.

Her ex for ten tranquil years.

After all this time, he should not have felt so familiar but, oh dear, he did. She knew the scent of that body and its lean, muscular strength. She knew its heat and its slick power and every response it could draw from hers.

She also recognized the ease with which he'd taken control of the moment and the decisiveness of his deep voice when it rumbled close to her ear. "I have a car waiting outside. Is this your only luggage?"

Kimberley nodded. "I assume you will tell me," she said tightly, "what this welcome party is all about."

"Not while the welcome party is within earshot. No."

Barking a request for the cameramen to stand aside

Perrini took her hand and pulled her into step with his ground-eating stride. Kimberley let him, because he was right, damn his arrogant, Italian-suited hide. Despite the speed with which he whisked her across the airport terminal, she could almost feel the hot breath of the pursuing media on her back.

This was neither the time nor the place for explanations. Inside his car, however, she would get answers.

Now that the initial shock had been blown away—by the haste of their retreat, by the heat of her gathering indignation, by the rush of adrenaline fired by Perrini's presence and the looming verbal battle—her brain was starting to tick over. This had to be her father's doing. And if it was a Howard Blackstone publicity ploy, then it had to be about Blackstone Diamonds, the company that ruled his life.

The knowledge made her chest tighten with a familiar ache of disillusionment.

She'd known her father would be flying in from Sydney for today's opening of the newest in his chain of exclusive, high-end jewelry boutiques. The opulent shopfront sat adjacent to the rival business where Kimberley worked. No coincidence, she thought bitterly, just as it was no coincidence that Ric Perrini was here in Auckland ushering her to his car.

Perrini was Howard Blackstone's right-hand man, second in command at Blackstone Diamonds, a legacy of his short-lived marriage to the boss's daughter. No doubt her father had sent him to fetch her; the question was *why?*

* * * * *

REQUEST YOUR FREE BOOKS!

2 FREE NOVELS PLUS 2 FREE GIFTS!

Silhouette® Desire®

Passionate, Powerful, Provocative!

YES! Please send me 2 FREE Silhouette Desire® novels and my 2 FREE gifts. After receiving them, if I don't wish to receive any more books, I can return the shipping statement marked "cancel." If I don't cancel, I will receive 6 brand-new novels every month and be billed just $3.80 per book in the U.S., or $4.47 per book in Canada, plus 25¢ shipping and handling per book and applicable taxes, if any*. That's a savings of almost 15% off the cover price! I understand that accepting the 2 free books and gifts places me under no obligation to buy anything. I can always return a shipment and cancel at any time. Even if I never buy another book from Silhouette, the two free books and gifts are mine to keep forever.

225 SDN EEXJ   326 SDN EEXU

Name	(PLEASE PRINT)	
Address		Apt.
City	State/Prov.	Zip/Postal Code

Signature (if under 18, a parent or guardian must sign)

Mail to the Silhouette Reader Service™:
IN U.S.A.: P.O. Box 1867, Buffalo, NY 14240-1867
IN CANADA: P.O. Box 609, Fort Erie, Ontario L2A 5X3

Not valid to current Silhouette Desire subscribers.

Want to try two free books from another line?
Call 1-800-873-8635 or visit www.morefreebooks.com.

* Terms and prices subject to change without notice. NY residents add applicable sales tax. Canadian residents will be charged applicable provincial taxes and GST. This offer is limited to one order per household. All orders subject to approval. Credit or debit balances in a customer's account(s) may be offset by any other outstanding balance owed by or to the customer. Please allow 4 to 6 weeks for delivery.

Your Privacy: Silhouette is committed to protecting your privacy. Our Privacy Policy is available online at www.eHarlequin.com or upon request from the Reader Service. From time to time we make our lists of customers available to reputable firms who may have a product or service of interest to you. If you would prefer we not share your name and address, please check here. ☐

SDES

nocturne™

Jachin Black always knew he was an outcast.
Not only was he a vampire, he was a vampire
banished from the Sanguinas society. Jachin, forced
to survive among mortals, is determined to buy
his way back into the clan one day.

Ariel Swanson, debut author of a vampire novel, could
be the ticket he needs to get revenge and take his
rightful place among the Sanguinas again. However,
the unsuspecting mortal woman has no idea of the
dark and sensual path she will be forced to travel.

Look for

RESURRECTION: THE BEGINNING

by

PATRICE MICHELLE

Available January 2008 wherever you buy books.

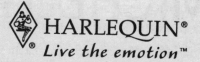

COMING NEXT MONTH

#1843 VOWS & A VENGEFUL GROOM—
Bronwyn Jameson
Diamonds Down Under
When a scandal overwhelms the opening of his latest diamond boutique, this millionaire proposes that his ex-lover be by his side—not only in the boardroom and the bedroom...but as his wife!

#1844 THE TEXAN'S CONTESTED CLAIM—
Peggy Moreland
A Piece of Texas
He was Texas's wealthiest and most eligible bachelor—and he was also about to uncover the past she'd kept hidden.

#1845 THE GREEK TYCOON'S SECRET HEIR—
Katherine Garbera
Sons of Privilege
To fulfill his father's dying wish, the Greek tycoon must marry the woman who betrayed him years ago. But his soon-to-be-wife has a secret that could rock more than his passion for her.

#1846 WHAT THE MILLIONAIRE WANTS...
—Metsy Hingle
This corporate raider thinks he's targeted his next big acquisition, until he meets the feisty beauty out to save her family's hotel. But what the millionaire wants...

#1847 BLACK SHEEP BILLIONAIRE—Jennifer Lewis
The billionaire's found the perfect way to exact his revenge on the woman who turned him away years ago. Let the seduction begin!

#1848 THE CORPORATE RAIDER'S REVENGE—
Charlene Sands
Seduce his business rival's daughter and gain information on his latest takeover. It was the perfect plan,..until the raider discovers his lover is pregnant.

SDCNM1206